KU-467-206

The Strange Tale
of
Barnabus
Kwerk

Erika McGann

illustrated by Phillip Cullen

THE O'BRIEN PRESS
DUBLIN

First published 2022 by
The O'Brien Press Ltd,
12 Terenure Road East, Rathgar,
Dublin 6, D06 HD27, Ireland.
Tel: +353 1 4923333; Fax: +353 1 4922777
E-mail: books@obrien.ie
Website: obrien.ie
The O'Brien Press is a member of Publishing Ireland.

ISBN: 978-1-78849-347-5
Text © copyright Erika McGann 2022
The moral rights of the author have been asserted.
Copyright for typesetting, layout, editing, design © The O'Brien Press Ltd
Design and layout by Emma Byrne.
Illustrations by Phillip Cullen.

All rights reserved.
No part of this publication may be reproduced
or utilised in any form or by any means,
electronic or mechanical, including photocopying,
recording or in any information storage
and retrieval system, without permission
in writing from the publisher.

1 3 5 7 8 6 4 2
22 24 26 25 23

Printed and bound in Great Britain by Clays Ltd, Elcograf S.p.A.

The paper in this book is produced using pulp from managed forests.

The Strange Tale of Barnabus Kwerk
receives financial assistance from
the Arts Council.

For Darius,

on his own big adventure this year

Acknowledgements

Thanks again to Phillip for his incredible illustrations, which have
really brought the book to life. To my editor, Nicola Reddy,
with whom it's always a joy to work. And to designer Emma Byrne
and everyone at The O'Brien Press.

DUNDEE CITY
COUNCIL

LOCATION

CENTRAL CHILDREN'S

ACCESSION NUMBER

C01 085 235X

SUPPLIER   PRICE

ASKEWS   £7·99

CLASS   DATE

            8·11·22

Contents

CHAPTER ONE

THE KWERKS

Not far from here, beyond the houses and the supermarket and the motorway and the trees, there's a quiet little town called Undle. Don't bother looking it up, it doesn't appear on any map. It should do (all towns and villages and cities should), but Undle doesn't.

The reason Undle doesn't appear on any map is not because it is invisible – far from it – it's because of the Kwerks.

The Kwerks have lived in Undle for as long as anyone can remember, and they are absurdly, horribly, filthily rich. They live in a great big house on the top of a hill in the middle of town, where they can look down their noses at the people below. The Big House on the hill is not a very nice one (much like the people inside it). It began as a rather sensible home built of wood, but as the Kwerk family fortune grew, every generation added a new wing or floor, each more garish and gaudy than the last. There are columns and buttresses made of silver and bronze, arches of sapphire and platinum-flecked turrets. There are emerald spires and ruby-chipped bricks, with pink diamond windows and pearl-covered sills. It's a ridiculous house. A preposterous house. And a dreadful eyesore for the people of Undle.

Although the Kwerks like others to know how very wealthy they are, they hate being asked for money. As the richest family around, they used to be plagued by people collecting for charity, day in and day out. They tried being rude, but that didn't work. They bought fierce snarling dogs, but the charity workers weren't afraid. They set booby traps and built a moat and poured boiling oil from the upper windows, but still the collectors came. So in the end, the Kwerks paid to have Undle wiped completely off the map. How could the charity workers find them if they couldn't find the town? And that is why you will never find Undle in any atlas.

On the morning our story begins, Barnabus Kwerk is shimmying down a rope made out of a knotted sheet that hangs from the dusty attic window of the Big House. He is on his way to school.

Barnabus is nine years old, smaller than average for his age, with a mop of dark curls and eyes halfway between green and grey. His clothes are chosen for him – sombre shirts and tailored trousers – to suit his dour relatives. However, Barnabus is an oddity among the Kwerks, being the only one in the family (and it is a very large family) who has no interest in money and no head for business. Since the day he was born he's been shown graphs and charts and spreadsheets, he's been told how much things cost and how much more money can be made. But Barnabus doesn't understand why the Kwerks want more money, just so it can pile up like mountains inside a giant vault. Wouldn't it be better used to help people? Barnabus asked his Uncle

Horace that question at dinner once – he got slapped over the head with a large trout and sent to the attic with no dessert.

Over the years Barnabus has tried many routes out of his attic room to get to school, but none of them have been successful to date. He got the sheet-rope idea from an adventure book he just finished reading. Barnabus is not permitted to read books. Any books found in his room or on his person are burned in one of the grand fireplaces of the house, and Barnabus is forced to copy out spreadsheets as punishment. Despite this, Barnabus still manages to get hold of books (you'll learn how a little later – it's heartwarming and quite interesting) and he manages to keep those books hidden from his family (you'll learn how he does this later too, and it's *very* interesting).

Barnabus tries not to look down as he slides from knot to knot on the sheet rope (the ground is very far away), instead looking over his shoulder at the yellow-brick school building in the distance. He can see some children arriving early, kissing or hugging their parents goodbye, running into the school yard, swinging on the swings. Barnabus *can't wait* to have a go on the swings.

But it won't happen today.

A strong hand clamps around his ankle. The housekeeper, Brunhilda, is leaning halfway out of a third-floor window.

'Where d'ya think you're going?'

'To school,' says Barnabus. 'I don't think Uncle Horace will mind.'

'Then why aren't you using the front door?'

'Em ...'

Brunhilda whips Barnabus in through the window so he lands on the floor with a smack.

'What do people go to school for, hmm?' she says, dragging him by the leg. 'To get a job and get rich, that's what for. You don't need schooling, you're already rich.'

'That's not why people go to sch–'

'Enough of that.' Brunhilda slides him into the nearest bathroom like a hockey puck. 'Clean yourself up, you smelly lump. Your uncle's taking you to see

Great-Aunt Claudia.'

Barnabus holds on tight to the bathroom sink. The only Kwerk scarier than Uncle Horace is Great-Aunt Claudia.

* * *

The north-east wing is floor-to-ceiling black marble. It's like standing in a cold, dark tomb. Barnabus would prefer to be in a tomb. His breath comes out in misty clouds and a shiver runs up his spine. Uncle Horace stands next to him – a tall, thin man in a pinstripe suit, his black hair slicked to his skull with greasy hair gel.

Normally Barnabus is terrified of his uncle. But the fear of Great-Aunt Claudia is briefly overshadowing the fear of Uncle Horace. As he does in all moments of discomfort or distress, Barnabus thinks of one of his favourite books and silently relives the story. In his mind he is sailing on a ship, part of a great race across the ocean, and it softens the thundering pounding in his chest just a little.

Uncle Horace seems almost as nervous as his nephew. He keeps smoothing the skinny moustache on his upper lip with his finger and thumb.

'You're to keep your trap shut,' he says, without looking at Barnabus. 'Not a word out of you, you little insect. Got it?'

'Yes, Uncle Horace.'

The heavy oak doors finally creak open to reveal a long hall of more black marble. At the end of it, seated on a large throne, is the eldest member of the Kwerk family.

When receiving visitors, Great-Aunt Claudia wears a towering orange wig and a corseted dress with the most enormous skirt you could ever imagine. When she sits on her throne, the skirt puffs up to her chin and spreads out to touch the walls on either side. She is actually Barnabus's great-great-great-aunt, and terrifically old, but for the sake of saving time everyone in the family refers to her as Great-Aunt Claudia.

Barnabus follows his uncle down the marble hallway. He can see the twinkle of the huge diamond nose plugs that Great-Aunt Claudia keeps wedged up each nostril. *To protect her precious sense of smell*, Uncle Horace once told him. They look dreadfully uncomfortable.

'This the brat?' the woman says.

(Because of the nose plugs, Great-Aunt Claudia's voice always sounds pinched, so she actually says, 'Dis de mrat?')

'Yes, Great-Aunt Claudia,' says Uncle Horace.

'Is he useless?'

'Utterly,' Uncle Horace replies.

Barnabus is petrified of the ancient woman on her throne. She looks like a giant, angry shrew and smells like the mouldy corner of the attic where the damp gets in. But this might be his only chance.

'I'm not useless, Great-Aunt Claudia. Really. If I could just go to school–'

A thin hand snaps over his mouth.

'*Useless*, Great-Aunt Claudia,' Uncle Horace says quickly. 'The boy is worth less than a rabbit's droppings.'

The old woman growls, her piercing eyes like drill bits. 'So this is it then, is it?' she says. 'A house full of good-for-nothings, and the very last heir is as worthless as the rest of you.'

'The business is doing very well,' says Uncle Horace. 'With my clever investments we've made more money this year than–'

'Business? *Investments*?' Great-Aunt Claudia's voice booms around the marble walls. She roughly twists a diamond plug in its nostril, and her face grows red through the thick white powder on her cheeks. 'Useless good-for-nothing! *Gold*, you pathetic dim-witted weasel, *gold*. You're all good-for-nothing cos you can't find *GOLD*.'

Uncle Horace remains silent as the old woman glares at him. Finally, she speaks again. 'Not one of you is fit to bear the name of Kwerk. And when you all die off, this useless brat will be the last to inherit.' She looks as if the thought of it makes her sick. 'There is only one thing to be done. I'm going to have to live forever.'

'My dear great-aunt,' says Uncle Horace, bowing slightly with an uncomfortable smile, 'of course you'll live for many more years. And we're all delighted about it. But perhaps we should discuss the details of your will, for when the time *does* come ... many, many years from now. I understand control of the business will be shared between the eldest five of us, but if you were to leave me completely in charge–'

'Useless cockroach!' the woman shrieks. 'You'll never be in charge. Cos I'll never die. Hear that, you useless waste of an ugly suit? I'm going to live forever. Forever and ever and ever and ever and EVER!'

Great-Aunt Claudia dies that night.

In the days that follow, Barnabus's life takes a very strange turn.

CHAPTER TWO

A POSTHUMOUS PARTY

The wind is howling, and the attic is cold. Barnabus sits at the circular window that frames the storm. He's been locked in the attic since Great-Aunt Claudia died.

'So you don't get in the way, you little worm,' Uncle Horace said as he turned the key in the lock.

It would be a particularly grim evening for Barnabus were it not for the new book he received moments before the rain began. You were promised a heartwarming and quite interesting explanation of where Barnabus gets his books, so here goes.

It's a mystery. There. Now you know. Intrigued? So is Barnabus.

His first ever book arrived by slingshot (Barnabus assumes it was a slingshot or something like it – how else could a book be fired through the open attic window of a very tall house?), and it missed his head by mere centimetres. Barnabus might have thought it some bizarre murder attempt had not the book been so marvellous. Only a good and kind person could have sent him something so marvellous. It was called *Practica Prenville and the Sweet Shop Villain*, and Barnabus devoured it in one night.

The second book – *Giraffes and the Secrets They Keep* – arrived the following week by the same means. The third was left under the cushion of his chair at the dinner table, the fourth under his towel at bathtime. Books have arrived at regular intervals ever since, often through the attic window, sometimes hidden in other places, and Barnabus hasn't a clue who sends them. He has his suspicions though.

There's a quiet chauffeur who doesn't snap at Barnabus

as often as others do; an assistant cook who didn't yell at him when he accidentally knocked over a pot while carrying his dirty dishes to the kitchen sink; and a maid who once smiled at him for no reason at all. But Barnabus's money is currently on the gardener as the mysterious book-gifter.

A short, gruff woman, the gardener has access to equipment that could be adapted for use as a slingshot. And one time she distracted the housekeeper, Brunhilda, when Barnabus dropped a small book that had been secreted in his coat pocket. The gardener happened to be standing by the open front door and let out the most enormous belch you could imagine, just as the book struck the tiled floor. Brunhilda spun around, repulsed by the horrific sound and the pungent scent that followed, and snarled at her.

'Oof,' the gruff woman said in reply, rubbing her belly and letting out a trail of smaller, lesser burps. 'That's the garlic from lunch popping up to say hello. Repeats on me something awful.'

Whoever the book-gifter is, Barnabus is beyond

grateful. To have the books is wonderful, but far, far better is the knowledge that someone out there cares for him. Someone out there does incredibly kind things, just for the sake of being kind, and expects nothing in return. Someone out there is willing to risk their job and the ire of the Kwerks so that one small boy can have some comfort and entertainment in this dark and lonely house. On the coldest and saddest of nights – and Barnabus has plenty of those – that thought keeps him warm and toasty in his bed.

As it happens, your narrator is also extremely grateful to the mysterious book-gifter. Because without the little bit of heart and humanity that those books bring, Barnabus Kwerk might not be the kind and curious boy he is today. He might eventually have succumbed to the meanness all around him and become a willing part of the cruel Kwerk empire. And then what sort of story would be left to tell? Certainly not one that most of us would like to read.

We've gotten a little sidetracked, dear reader, so let's get back to Barnabus sitting in the attic window some time after his Great-Aunt Claudia's death.

Outside, lightning flashes from dark clouds and the rain swirls around in little tornadoes. It's a bit scary, but Barnabus wishes he could be out there in it, chasing the storm and stamping in puddles. He imagines himself as a character from one of his books; a scientist perhaps, studying the electricity that zaps to the ground. Or an artist, painting a canvas in shades of dark blue with splashes of white. He could be a rescuer, saving a puppy from the cliff's edge before it's swept into the sea. Or maybe a pilot, braving the stormy weather in his amazing flying machine.

Barnabus clings to the book in his hands – a well-worn copy of *The Time I Met a Yeti* – because he'll probably never be any of those things. Not if Uncle Horace has his way. Barnabus is a Kwerk, and Kwerks only do one thing: make money.

At this moment, the whole family is downstairs planning Great-Aunt Claudia's funeral. From the noise that drifts to the top of the house, it sounds more like a party. Aunt Gladys laughs like she's got

the worst hiccups in the world; Cousin Armand bellows for the housekeeper every time his glass is empty (Armand wouldn't get up unless his seat was on fire, and maybe not even then); Uncle Clarence coughs and hacks so hard it sounds like he might throw up his own feet (that's thanks to the stinking pipe that sits forever on his lower lip); and Aunt Reba keeps ordering the others to join her in singing old shanty songs that no-one knows the words to, Reba included. There's cheering and shouting and general merriment, and Barnabus can't help feeling a little bit sorry for Great-Aunt Claudia.

He finds a comfier spot on the windowsill and turns the next page of his book, when through the window he spots someone coming up the hill.

People don't call to the Big House uninvited (the Kwerks have been known to use electric cattle prods on those who do), but the stranger walks through the iron gates and up the winding driveway as if the house is her own. The fierce guard dogs don't bark or bite – they lower their ears as she strolls past. Barnabus doesn't know anyone outside of the family and the staff, but there is something familiar about this woman. She is very tall and very thin, and she carries no umbrella so her long, black hair is drenched and hangs like curtains over her face. Her woollen jumper is old and worn, and she has a rucksack on her back that appears to be full of sticks. When she reaches the door, Barnabus can no longer see her, but he hears the *BAUM, BAUM, BAUM* of the knocker and the sudden silence of the party below. *BAUM, BAUM, BAUM*, the knocker goes again.

Eventually the door is opened and light spills onto the driveway. When the door closes again, Barnabus can't hear any more.

CHAPTER THREE

THE STRANGER IN THE BIG HOUSE

In his attempts to escape to school, Barnabus has never made it beyond the grounds of the Big House. (He got close to the gates once, but he was spotted from an upstairs window and the dogs were set on him – he was dragged back by his collar with his jumper soaked in doggy drool.) However, getting out of the attic has never been a problem. A mishmash of design, the Big House is full of vents and hatches and forgotten, blocked-up openings. There's a secret maze inside the walls, and Barnabus is the clever mouse that knows every route.

Desperate to find out more about the stranger who has just arrived, Barnabus quickly piles rickety pieces of furniture on top of each other – the chair onto the desk, the stool onto the chair, the floor lamp onto the stool – and scurries up like a squirrel climbing a tree. Balanced on the lampshade, he peels back a corner of the faded pink wallpaper to reveal a rusty grate. It comes open with a squeak, and Barnabus climbs inside.

If upon reading the phrase 'secret maze' you immediately thought, 'That's where Barnabus hides his books!', then there are no flies on you, clever reader. There are indeed dozens and dozens of books hidden within the walls of the Big House. The secret maze is punctuated by piles of hardbacks and paperbacks taped to solid structures. (Those of you who are precious about how your books are kept might be appalled, but when those books are at risk of being burned should they go sliding down a vent and shooting from a loose grate into the face of an ill-tempered Kwerk, then a bit of duct tape is really the lesser of two evils.)

You may want to skip this very next bit if you're the sort of person who doesn't like small spaces, because Barnabus Kwerk has no problem with small spaces. He crawls into a vent no wider than his shoulders and no taller than a small boy on all fours. It's dark and cold, and strange sounds creep through the metal so it seems like the walls are whispering to each other. Barnabus isn't afraid; he knows it's just the sound of the house moving as it heats and cools in different places. (All houses move – it's just so slight you can't see it – and the Big House is so big it moves more than most.)

Barnabus knows the route to the drawing room, where the Kwerk funeral-planning party is taking place. Picking his way over stuck-down books, he'll go left when he hits the wall straight ahead, then down a steep chute until he smells something vinegary, and then to the right until the air feels cloudy. He'll pass a grate that stinks of socks (that's Cousin Laurel's bedroom) and another that smells of sweat (that's the sauna). He'll need to squeeze through a tiny hole until he hears the sound of dishes, and then down again until it's hot. He'll be right next to the drawing room's chimney then, and through a gap in the brick he'll be able to hear what's going on.

But Barnabus doesn't get that far, because just as the

air gets cloudy, he catches a whiff of something unexpected – a burnt-rubber smell, like that of just-poured tar. And he can hear voices coming from Uncle Horace's office.

'... totally uninvited. You've got some nerve.'

'She was my great-aunt too. I'm simply paying my respects. Oh, for heaven's sake, Horace, flare those nostrils any harder and they'll pop right off your face.'

Barnabus slides up a vertical vent and braces his hands and feet against the walls, where he can see through the grate into Uncle Horace's office.

His uncle is there, pacing in front of his big oak desk. The stranger is there too. Loose threads hang from holes in her woollen jumper and her boots are heavy and well worn. She is in stark contrast to Uncle Horace and his immaculate pinstripe suit, and yet the two share similarities as well. They are both tall and narrow in the face, though the woman's grey eyes have an openness and intensity that Uncle Horace's lack.

She stands to one side as the man paces back and forth, and Barnabus thinks it is she who smells so strange – that scent of burnt rubber. He smelled something like it when the driveway of the Big House was being resurfaced.

'While I'm here,' the stranger continues, 'I want to spend some time with the boy.'

Uncle Horace smirks. 'So that's your game, Jemima. You're hoping the brat's got the gift. Well, he doesn't. He's as useless as—'

'His biscuit spoon of an uncle? I don't doubt it. But his mother was my twin sister after all. I owe her at least a passing interest in the child.'

Jemima turns her back on Uncle Horace to pick up her rucksack full of sticks, and he bristles at the rudeness. 'Oh, *now* you owe Sylvia,' he says, which makes her pause. 'Didn't seem that way when you took off gallivanting and left her to rot.'

The woman's eyes burn with grey fire. 'Syl believed she could make the Kwerks a decent family again. I knew better. And I had no desire to stay in this wretched house and watch her prove me right.'

Uncle Horace is smiling now. 'Please do stay for the

funeral, sister. Pay your respects to our dearly departed great-aunt. But you're not going anywhere near Sylvia's brat. And once the old bag is in the ground, I never want to see your ugly face again. Understood?'

Jemima seems to compose herself. 'Honestly, Horace, I've had bowel infections I've missed more than you. So, yes. Please. Let's never meet again.'

Barnabus doesn't see the woman leave Uncle Horace's office. He slides down the vent until he's sitting at the bottom in the cold, cloudy air.

I had a mother, he thinks.

He always presumed he had a mother at some point, but no-one has ever mentioned her. Now it's definite. He had a mother. And his mother had a twin sister. And his mother's twin sister wants to meet him.

Barnabus feels something strange in his chest – it's warm and soft, and it spreads through his limbs. He crawls back to his attic bedroom and climbs into bed. It's a long time before he feels sleepy. *I had a mother*, he thinks as he finally drifts off, feeling that warm sensation tingle to the ends of his fingers and toes.

CHAPTER FOUR

THE FUNERAL

The Kwerks have their own cemetery. It's in the grounds of the Big House.

Generations ago they decided to have their own cemetery, in part so they wouldn't have to be buried alongside the lowly people of Undle, but mostly because Undle Town Cemetery has limits on how big your gravestone can be.

Cornelius Kwerk was the first of the Kwerks to be filthily rich – that was very many years ago now. He wanted to make sure that everyone knew how horribly rich he was, even after his death. So he stated in his will that his gravestone should be at least twice the size of any gravestone currently in existence in Undle. Years later his daughter, Fatima Kwerk, demanded that *her* gravestone be at least *three* times the size of her father's. On and on it went through the generations until the cemetery stretching down the hill from the Big House became littered with increasingly huge monuments, horrible statues and ghastly mausoleums.

The giant stone angel that is Great-Aunt Claudia's monument threatens to block out the sun. It requires three cranes to lift it into place.

Next to the gravesite are rows of wooden chairs. The entire Kwerk family is seated there, all dressed in black with dark-coloured umbrellas. Barnabus is in the front row. Uncle Horace and Aunt Gladys sit either side of him. Several times during the morning he has caught the scent of just-poured tar, and turned, hoping to catch a glimpse of his mysterious Aunt Jemima. He has never heard anyone talk to Uncle Horace the way she did, and Barnabus is eager to meet her. But the other Kwerks have kept him surrounded since breakfast. Before sitting down in the cemetery, all he has seen today has been a wall of black suits.

Now that the family is seated by the gravesite, everyone looks uneasy. It's because of Great-Aunt Claudia's gargantuan monument. There is no lightning or thunder today, but gale-force winds are blowing hats off heads and turning umbrellas inside out, and the massive stone angel sways over the open grave like a wrecking ball with wings.

The funeral celebrant doesn't look too happy about it either. She stands to the side, keeping one eye on the great swinging angel overhead as she speed-reads a very untrue account of Great-Aunt Claudia's life. 'Intelligent, quick-witted and unfailingly generous, Claudia led an exemplary life. She was an accomplished woman who appreciated good music and …'

One of the cranes creaks alarmingly. Barnabus notices that the rope wrapped around the angel's left arm is frayed. He leans forward to get a closer look. The rope is not just frayed – it's been cut. There's a clean cut through the rope so that only a few strands are left intact. And they're starting to snap.

'Uncle Horace.'

'Shush, you little snot,' his uncle hisses.

'But I think—'

'I said shush if you know what's good for you!'

Looking very worried, the celebrant is now racing to the end of the service.

'Would anyone like to say a few words about Claudia before we finish?'

'Get on with it!' someone shouts from the back row.

'Very well,' says the celebrant. 'In that case I'd like to—'

Eeeerwwwuuurrrk-PING!

The cut rope snaps, and the huge stone angel comes flying towards the wooden seats. The celebrant dives into the grave, barely avoiding the angel's feet before they smash a splintery path through the just-emptied rows of seats.

Barnabus throws himself to the ground. He can see shadows in the grass – the Kwerks diving and sprinting in all directions as the great hunk of stone continues to swing and crash its way through the funeral party. Ahead of him one figure stands still, watching the commotion. It's Aunt Jemima.

Calmly, she takes her rucksack from her back and shakes out the collection of sticks. Barnabus stares in wonder as she quickly fits them together to form something big and triangular. In a flash she hooks some colourful cloth to the corners and spins the contraption over her shoulders. It's a hang glider – Barnabus saw a picture of one in a book once.

Aunt Jemima stands in the frame underneath the sail, holding tight to the bar in front. Her pale-grey eyes look directly at Barnabus, and she starts running. The wind is batting the sail from left and right, but Aunt Jemima barrels through. She is running straight at Barnabus.

She's going to crash into me, Barnabus thinks, *or run over me.*

Still on the ground, he starts inching backwards. The woman's intense grey eyes never leave him for a moment. She's coming at him very fast, and the sail is lifting her feet from the ground as she runs.

Suddenly Barnabus hears Uncle Horace scream over the wind. 'Stop her! She's after the brat. *Stop her!*'

The Kwerks swarm in Aunt Jemima's direction, but

they're too late. As Barnabus gets to his feet, the colour-ful sail swoops down on him like a giant bird. A strap drops over his head, cinching in at his waist, and sud-denly he's airborne, moving up with the wind towards the dark clouds.

'No! *No!*' Uncle Horace continues screaming, but his voice fades away as Barnabus is lifted higher and higher into the sky.

He feels like a spider in a sink when the tap is turned on, but instead of being swirled down into the drain, he's being swirled up into the clouds. Far below, the Kwerks look like ants in black suits, racing back and forth across the cemetery, and Great-Aunt Claudia's stone angel lies in the grass, looking regular-sized from this distance. Barnabus can spot Uncle Horace among the ants. The man is glaring at the hang glider in fury. Barnabus lifts a hand and gives him a little wave. It feels delightfully cheeky. The Kwerks continue to shrink to nothing, like the memory of a nightmare when you wake in daylight. Then suddenly,

WHOOSH.

The hang glider swoops and loops and spins, tossed around in the gales, with Barnabus swinging wildly underneath. The strap around his waist starts to hurt. As if reading his mind, Aunt Jemima looks down at him, yelling through the noise of the wind, 'Your breakfast getting squeezed out your ears, is it? Not to worry, we'll land soon.'

Along with the belly-pinching of the strap, Barnabus is also starting to feel quite sick. 'Aunt Jemima ...' he groans.

'Just a few more seconds,' the woman replies.

Another gust of wind catches the hang glider, push-ing it beyond the limits of Undle, then it is suddenly hurtling towards the earth. Barnabus sees a dense forest coming towards him at alarming speed. He squeezes his eyes shut and holds his breath, waiting to hit the branches. But there's a sudden lift instead, and he feels his feet gently touch the ground.

CHAPTER FIVE

A NICE LITTLE TOURIST SPOT

'Half thought I'd get you skewered on a pointy gravestone, but that went quite well.' Aunt Jemima is digging the tight strap out of the folds of Barnabus's blazer. 'If you'd like to vomit, now's the time.'

Barnabus declines. He doesn't know whether to laugh or cry. His legs feel like jelly and his mouth is dry. There are trees all around. New trees, *different* trees, ones he has not seen from his attic window. The ground under his feet is soft and wet, with curling weeds and brambles and muck. There are no manicured lawns and square-cut hedges, and no-one is shouting 'Get off the grass, you little snot!' or 'Get back to your room!' Barnabus looks up at the windblown clouds.

I was up there, he thinks. *I flew through the sky.*

Relieved and excited and frightened and sick, it all churns in Barnabus's belly like a washing machine.

The strap around his waist is gone and Aunt Jemima swiftly pulls him to his feet. 'No time for pleasantries, I'm afraid,' she says, 'so I'll do this quickly. I'm your Aunt Jemima. I doubt I'm ever mentioned in that house – I left that dreadful place a long time ago. I had presumed you'd be a money-grabbing weasel by now, being raised by Horace and Gladys, but I've since heard otherwise. I've also heard you're not attending school, is that right?'

Still reeling, Barnabus nods. 'I'm not allowed.'

'Well, that'll be remedied soon enough. *If* you want to come with me, that is.' Aunt Jemima grabs the hang glider and begins pulling it apart. 'I realise this was technically a kidnapping, but it was the only chance I had to get you out of there, and I couldn't get near you this morning to ask what you'd prefer. So if you'd like to return to the Big House, say so now and I'll drop you back immediately. No harm, no foul. If, however, you'd like to leave the Big House forever and come with me, then we need to move quickly.'

Things are indeed moving quickly. Barnabus has never even left the grounds of the Big House before, and here he is, standing in a forest, free of Uncle Horace and the others. But this woman is a complete stranger. And she still has that odd smell, as if her clothes are made of burning rubber.

'Are you taking me to my mother?' Barnabus asks hopefully.

Aunt Jemima flinches and doesn't meet his eye. 'No,' she says. 'No, I'm afraid your mother is gone.'

Barnabus feels a sinking in his chest. He watches in silence as the woman stuffs the sticks back into her rucksack. Finally she looks up and says, 'It's now or never, little plum.'

Barnabus decides it's now. 'I'll come with you.'

'Marvellous.' Aunt Jemima smiles. 'Now let's get moving. Horace will have a search party out in minutes, and if we're late to the Botanical Gardens the tour guide will be giving me daggers.'

* * *

Barnabus is puzzled by his aunt's last statement, and when they emerge from the woods exhausted from running and out of breath, he finally asks, 'Why are we going to the Botanical Gardens?'

'It's our way out,' Aunt Jemima replies. 'Or really our way *in*. I'll explain as we go. Quick, off with that jacket. I've got a jumper here that should fit you.'

She stuffs the black blazer Barnabus wore for Great-Aunt Claudia's funeral into her rucksack, exchanging it for a pale-blue woollen jumper, worn to holes in places. Barnabus barely has it over his head before she's shoving a pair of sunglasses onto his face, hanging an old-fashioned camera around his neck, and topping off the look with a large-brimmed straw hat.

'What's all this for?' he asks.

'Disguise,' his aunt says, donning a sunhat and a pair of binoculars. 'From here on, we're tourists. Try to look interested.'

That won't be difficult. This is Barnabus's first time

in the outside world. Everything is fascinating to him. He gazes at the roadside flowers – daisies, buttercups, dandelions, the kind that you and I take for granted – because the groomed gardens of the Big House have only expensive, imported blooms. He is shushed by his aunt when he squeals with glee at the sight of a black and white animal scurrying into the undergrowth. 'Was that a badger?' he asks.

'Yes. Now, hush. Tourists aren't blown away by wild-flowers and rodents.'

'Badgers aren't rodents.' Barnabus is tickled to remember the fact from one of his hidden books. 'They're related to weasels and–'

'Less talking, more walking,' Aunt Jemima says. 'The tour's leaving any minute.'

They pass a few cottages with pretty gardens in front, a small shop, more cottages, and then a set of gates with 'Botanical Gardens' written in flowery bronze letters. Aunt Jemima throws her rucksack behind the gates on the way in, then hurries Barnabus towards a group of real tourists. A tour guide with a brightly coloured umbrella and a name badge that says 'Donal' scowls at the latecomers.

'Now that everyone is here,' Donal says, 'we can begin the tour. Please follow me to our first stop, the Playground of the Peonies, and feel free to ask questions. If you find yourself lost at any point, just look for the umbrella. Now …'

He turns, holding the umbrella high, and launches into a detailed description of the various species of peony.

'Aunt Jemima,' Barnabus whispers as the two of them drift to the back of the group, 'why are we here?'

'The tour's a front,' his aunt replies, 'for access to the Botanical Gardens' squidgy bit. Some of the guides let you sneak off right away, but Donal there is a cactus spine in the backside. He'll make us wait for the tea-rooms.'

'What's a squidgy bit?'

'It's our escape route.' Aunt Jemima looks up when she hears something that sounds like a large bee trapped in a jar. 'And it's going to be tight. If I'm not much mistaken, that's a helicopter coming.'

Barnabus feels a prickle of sweat down his back. 'Aunt Reba has a helicopter.'

'Ugh, Reba. I'd rather lick a used plaster than see her again.' Aunt Jemima pushes the camera around Barnabus's neck into his hands. 'Keep that in front of your face and pretend to take pictures. They'll have people coming in by road and through the fields around this place too. Probably with heat sensors and heart sensors and whatever spy gear is new these days. Don't make it easy for them to spot you.'

Barnabus follows his aunt's example, crisscrossing over the pathways, pretending to be engrossed in this border of red flowers and that circle of yellow ones. At any other time he would actually be engrossed, but the bee-in-a-jar sound is getting louder and he is too nervous to notice the flora.

He does, however, notice a couple of tourists among the group who seem as uninterested in the Botanical Gardens as he is. The man and woman dawdle on the path, sniffing with bored expressions. The tourist in front of them grins and points to a clump of purple flowers.

'Have you ever seen blooms as perfect as that?' he asks.

The bored woman doesn't answer, her lip curling with distaste at such a silly thing in which to be interested. As the enthusiastic tourist moves on, the bored woman's companion pats her on the shoulder.

'Won't be much longer, Maura, my love. We're nearly to the glasshouses.'

'Donal and his bloody tours,' she replies. 'Loves the sound of his own voice.'

'I know, I know,' her companion says, patting her shoulder once more.

The two are dressed in very practical wear: jackets and trousers with many pockets, and comfortable hiking boots. They each have a set of binoculars and the woman has a camera, much like the one around Barnabus's neck.

'Aunt Jemima,' he says quietly to his aunt, 'I don't think those two are part of the normal tourist group either.'

His aunt glances at the pair. 'No, they're moth-watchers. They'll be heading for the squidgy bit too.'

'Moth-watchers?'

'They watch moths,' Aunt Jemima replies, as if that makes perfect sense. 'And they get in the way. Your average moth-watcher has all the sense nature gave a turnip. If it were up to me, they'd be banned. Ah, we're here at last. Keep up, now.'

Donal is indicating that the group gather around him by a gateway in a hedge.

'Now that we've reached the final stop on our tour, those of you with orange tickets will be following me to the Orchid Tearooms for complementary afternoon tea. For those of you with green tickets, your visit with us is at an end. Please exit the gardens here.'

He unlocks the gate as Aunt Jemima produces two green tickets from her pocket and the two moth-watchers impatiently push their way to the front. Once through the hedge the gate is locked behind them, and Barnabus realises it isn't an exit at all. They are, in fact, in a small, enclosed garden that is growing wild.

'Francis,' the first moth-watcher says, 'you go first and I'll follow.'

'Right you are, Maura, my love,' her companion replies.

He heads for a rocky bit of the garden, to a patch of thick moss. Standing squarely on the patch he begins to jump up and down. Oddly there appears to be a bit of spring to the mossy patch, and the man bounces higher and higher until,

Schlurrp.

He disappears, sucked right into the ground.

Barnabus cries out in fright, and Maura rolls her eyes at him before following the man through the moss in the same way.

'Aunt Jemima,' Barnabus's voice quivers as the moth-watcher is sucked out of sight, 'where are we going?'

His aunt places a hand on his shoulder and smiles. 'To the most wonderful place imaginable,' she says. 'To the centre of the Earth.'

CHAPTER SIX

THROUGH THE SQUIDGY BIT

'First time's always a bit fraught. Don't be embarrassed.'

Aunt Jemima nods encouragement as Barnabus stands on the mossy patch where the two moth-watchers vanished. His knees are trembling, and he can't keep the wobble out of his voice. 'But what happens after I go through the moss? Where do I come out? What do I do?'

'Don't worry about that,' his aunt replies. 'You just jump a few times and once you're through, gravity will take care of everything. I know it's a bit nerve-wracking on your first go but trust me, it's a hell of a ride. You'll love it.'

Barnabus doesn't believe her. He doesn't believe you can get to the centre of the Earth through a patch of moss. He doesn't like this at all. He's about to step off the patch and tell Aunt Jemima as much when the bee-in-a-jar sound returns with a vengeance. It is very loud, very close, enough to cause the leaves of the hedge to whip about in a tizzy.

'Quick!' Aunt Jemima cries. 'Through the squidgy bit, fast as you can. I'll be right behind you. Jump, little plum, *jump*!'

Terrified, as a big, black helicopter soars into view, Barnabus bounces on the mossy patch, jumping up and down on the spot, higher and higher as the springy bit of ground beneath him gives and gives and gives until ...

Schlurrp.

* * *

You'll love it.

Aunt Jemima was mistaken. Barnabus is hurtling

downwards, out of control, turning and rolling in a never-ending corkscrew tunnel, his stomach suddenly a frog caught on elastic – leaping into his throat, being snapped back down, then leaping again.

That kind of feeling can be brilliant for a few seconds, like when you fly down one of those winding slides at a fancy swimming pool. But when it lasts for more than a few seconds, it becomes less fun. When it goes on and on for many minutes, it becomes desperately unpleasant. That is how Barnabus is feeling.

He is also in complete darkness. The tunnel is pitch black, and the quiet of the Earth beneath the surface is unnerving. It is utter quiet. A totally-alone kind of quiet. Barnabus tries to call out to his aunt, but the fall is stealing the air right out of his lungs.

Time passes until finally there is light at the end of the tunnel. A very dim light, but light nonetheless. Barnabus speeds towards it. It grows and grows until – *FWITT* – he is shot from the tunnel, a human spitball from a straw, and keeps going.

'Use your feet, you eejit!' yells an impatient voice, but

Barnabus doesn't know what that means.

He speeds down a slide of polished rock which curves upwards like the curled antenna of a massive creepy-crawly. Barnabus can see where the antenna slide ends. He's going way too fast. When he reaches the end, he's going to fly off and–

SMACK.

Barnabus hits the rock wall back at the mouth of the tunnel and groans in pain.

'You'll want to move, sharpish,' the moth-watcher, Maura, says as she walks away.

Barnabus can hear a whistling in the tunnel. Or an alarm. He throws his body off to one side, just in time to avoid Aunt Jemima as she – *'Wahooooo!'* – comes careening from the darkness and soars over the polished rock. She uses her feet, pushing them against the lipped edges of the slide, reducing her speed. Instead of flying off the end of the curled antenna, she slows to a stop halfway, then slides comfortably back down.

'That never gets old!' she says, grinning. 'Honestly, it's the bat's bloomers. I love it.'

Barnabus doesn't agree. He'd take soaring through the air over plummeting through the ground any day. The nerves start to ease off within moments, however, and he can finally take a proper look at where he and his aunt have landed. The space is poorly lit – he can't see further than ten metres or so in any direction – but he can see that the antenna slide extends beyond a rocky ledge, on which he is sitting very close to the edge. He scoots back a bit. Above him there is total darkness, and below the ledge the same.

'Is this really the centre of the Earth?' he asks.

'It is.' Aunt Jemima seems excited. 'But this is not the good bit. I won't describe where we're going – I want you to see it for yourself.'

There are flights of stony steps at either end of the ledge, and Aunt Jemima takes the same route as the moth-watchers. The steps lead to a long wooden platform, suspended by ropes from a ceiling that Barnabus can't see. Aunt Jemima trots quickly down the platform to a connecting one beyond, then to the next, almost vanishing in the dim light provided by oil lamps that hang at regular intervals. Barnabus tries to hurry after her, but the dangling trail sways with each step.

'You'll get used to it,' his aunt calls back. 'Just keep to the middle. Don't want you falling off.'

Barnabus gulps, wanting to lie face down on the wooden path so there's no chance he'll go toppling off the side.

'Move with it,' Aunt Jemima says, demonstrating. 'Don't fight the swing.'

He reaches the next platform, taking small, careful steps, and slowly the swinging path settles.

'That's it,' the woman says, moving on. 'You've got it.'

Barnabus struggles to keep up with his aunt, following her along the wooden trail that weaves through the vast, cavernous space like a snake. Any time he loses sight of her in the gloom, the smell of her – that burnt-rubber scent, like a newly poured road – reassures him that she's still there. When there is a fork in the trail, he is able to stay with her by scent alone.

The pathway forks many times, and more paths appear above and below, a spiderweb of wooden trails criss-crossing through the cavern. A glowing dot appears in the distance and their route leads towards it.

Barnabus begins to walk with more confidence. Moving in time with the gently swinging path, as though to music, is becoming fun. And the awe he feels for the place he's in – the centre of the *Earth* – makes his body seem light as a feather.

The glowing dot grows as he and his aunt approach, and it gives the space a sense of warmth. Compared to the pale light of the oil lamps over the paths, the glow ahead is golden and full of welcome, like a cosy, crackling fireplace. As they get closer, it is the size of a basketball, then a car, then a house. When it is the size of the hill on which the Big House sits, Barnabus realises it is still some distance away. It must be gigantic. And it is making sound.

At first, it's just white noise, but as they get nearer Barnabus can hear the golden thing ticking and tocking and clicking and chiming. There is so much noise, it should be unpleasant. But it isn't. It's a sweet sound, that of a thousand heartbeats; fast ones, slow ones, loud ones, soft ones. All beating together to make one glorious melody.

The great, glowing ball seems the size of the moon now. It is filled with turning wheels and gears, like the inner workings of a clock. There are huge wheels and smaller pinions, circled with thick cogs and thin ones, the teeth catching and slipping as the gears turn together, with the mechanism making all those wonderful *tick-tock* sounds. Bells are struck with a lovely *ding*, and every piece shines in gleaming gold on this rippling, shimmering, ticking moon.

'What is this place?' Barnabus gasps.

Aunt Jemima smiles lovingly. 'This, my dear little plum, is the Clockwork.'

CHAPTER SEVEN

INSIDE THE CLOCKWORK

Great chains stretch from the globe like moon-beams, disappearing into the darkness of the cavern to connect to walls far beyond, while the hanging pathways wind their way in and out of the mechanism as though it's a splendid, golden apple riddled with lovely wooden worms.

'Are we going in there?' Barnabus asks.

'We most certainly are.'

He follows on his aunt's heels.

'What is this place? I mean, what is it for? How long has it been here? How is it here at all? Who built it?'

Aunt Jemima laughs. 'Well, I'm glad you're this

excited, because our family history is intertwined with this place. Like I said, it's called the Clockwork and it is the ticking heart of the planet. It literally makes the world go round. I've no idea who built it and I can't tell you how long it's been here, because nobody knows that. But I can tell you that we all rely on it. Without the Clockwork the Earth wouldn't turn, there'd be no night and there'd be no day, and none of us would survive.'

Barnabus is grinning from ear to ear. Everything around him looks and sounds so wonderful, and he has an overwhelming urge to touch the rotating teeth of the nearest gears and wheels.

'Don't even think about it,' his aunt says, though Barnabus hasn't so much as reached out a finger. 'Getting caught on a cog is a surefire way to fall off the path.'

Barnabus doesn't touch anything but nearly goes tumbling off the path when a shadow swoops down and something feathery brushes over his head.

'Agh!' he cries. 'What was that?'

Aunt Jemima glances back. 'Ah, that is what attracts

the moth-watchers,' she says. 'A frilly moth. Not dangerous to people, but do keep an eye out. They're everywhere and they're rather large. Two-metre wing-span when in flight.'

She points to one of the golden wheels and Barnabus sees something stuck to it that looks like a folded feather boa in light grey – another of the frilly moths. Its downy plumes dance with the tiniest movement in the air, and every once in while it shudders, sending a ripple through its feathery wings. Barnabus stares at the creature in wonder.

'It's amazing!'

Aunt Jemima snorts in amusement. 'I suppose it must be, when you're used to the small ones. We're not moth-watchers though, so less gawping, more walking.'

They move on. Barnabus gazes at the moth until it's out of sight, then goes back to watching the golden pieces of the Clockwork. He is thinking that he has never seen so much gold, but then he realises he has never really seen gold at all. Oddly, it is the only precious metal that is absent from the Big House.

He doesn't worry about losing Aunt Jemima now. He can still smell her. In fact, he can't *not* smell her. His aunt's hot-tar scent has grown considerably, exponentially, explosively. It has begun to assault his nostrils until the tiny hairs inside feel singed. Barnabus worries the smell might knock him right out of his shoes.

I wonder what it means, he thinks. *Might it mean she's ill? Perhaps I should mention it.*

But manners keep Barnabus's lips shut, and soon the overpowering scent starts to fade.

The lovely golden hue of the Clockwork is also fading. The gears and wheels are still there, but they have become duller, darker, slower. Some of them drip with thick black oil and others look like rusted iron. The glorious ticking sound has also changed. Where before it sang with the lightness of birds, now it squeaks and creaks with painful turns.

'What happened?' Barnabus asks. 'Where did all the lovely gold go?'

Aunt Jemima surveys the grim workings with sorrow. 'It's sick,' she says. 'Like much of the Clockwork these days. These sicker parts grow and spread. One day they'll be too big and there'll be too many of them.'

'And what happens then?'

'The Clockwork will die. And the Earth will be doomed.'

Barnabus shudders. 'What's making it sick?'

His aunt sighs. 'This sickness has been generations in the making. But it began with the Kwerks and their insatiable greed.'

The mention of his family and their obsession with money settles on Barnabus like a rain cloud. He doesn't want to know any more about that for now. He watches his feet and doesn't look up until a gentle golden hue begins to creep back into the light. He and Aunt Jemima are entering a healthier part of the ticking heart, and it lifts Barnabus's own heart like a warm summer's day.

They follow the wooden trail to a wide-open space, where the path curls around the area like ribbon wrapped around a ball. In the centre of this space, dozens of huge stones hang from thick golden chains – the bigger stones are cylindrical in shape, and the smaller ones are round. This place is buzzing with excitement and squeals of delight. People toddle along the boards, calling out to each other and ...

Barnabus blinks hard and looks again. They are not people. They are something else.

They have arms and legs and heads like people and they are quite round in shape, but there is something peculiar about their behinds. At first, Barnabus thinks that each is carrying a large rucksack that hangs uncomfortably at their bottoms, but looking again he can see the heavy rucksack-looking things, in fact, *are* their bottoms. Each of them has an enormous bottom that looks extremely heavy and almost sweeps the wooden boards as they walk.

This unusual appendage apparently makes walking quite difficult, and although they shuffle slowly over the path, they seem to do so joyfully and with great purpose. There are a number of wooden catapults positioned at various points along the trail, and the large-bottomed creatures all seem to be in a hurry to get to one. Once there, they push and scuffle with each other for the chance to sit in the catapult's bucket. (Imagine a raucous game of musical chairs involving a group of extraordinarily large four-year-olds and too few chairs, and you'll have it about right.) When one of the strange creatures is finally seated, others flop onto the front of the device and the catapult is fired.

'Haweeeeeee!' the creature cries, and Barnabus gasps to see it go careening through the air and smack right into one of the round boulders dangling in the middle of the space, sticking fast to the thing like a clump of wet tissue hitting a window.

'Haweeeeeee!'

Another creature hits the stone from the other side, then another and another.

'Haweeeeeee! Haweeeeeee! Haweeeeeee!'

With half a dozen or so clinging on, the boulder begins to sink with the weight of all those magnificent bottoms. As it sinks lower and lower, one of the bigger stones moves upwards. When the smaller stone seems to be at its lowest point, the creatures detach with a squeal of delight and land safely on a sheet of springy fabric stretched beneath the space.

'Oooooooway-ay-ay!'

There is no mistaking the unbridled glee in the creatures' voices, which swell and swirl like whale calls through the ocean.

Barnabus is wonderstruck. 'What is *this* place? And who are they?'

'This is a Weight Station,' his aunt replies. 'Do you know how a regular clock works?'

'Sort of. Every Saturday in the Big House Brunhilda opens the grandfather clock in the main hall and pulls on the chains so that the weights go back up to the top. If she forgets to do it, the clock stops running.'

'Well,' Aunt Jemima says, 'the Clockwork works in much the same way. Gleewatts – those delightful creatures currently springing through the air – pull down the smaller stones, each of which pulls up one of those mighty cylindrical weights. Then, just like your grandfather clock, gravity slowly pulls down the cylindrical weight and the wheel connected to its chain turns. That wheel turns the next wheel, and so on and so forth.

There are dozens of weights in dozens of Weight Stations powering the Clockwork at all times.'

'Does that mean the gleewatts can't take a break?'

'Ha! Just you try and make them. Gleewatts live for the thrill. It's all they want or think about. They do sleep – you see, there's a couple of them slumped on the path up there – but every waking moment is spent flying through the air, or hurrying to a catapult so they can fly through the air. There's no stopping them.'

'They do look happy.'

'They are. And they're generally very good-natured, but there are occasional scuffles over who's next to sit on a catapult. Sometimes a gleewatt will get pushed and come rolling down the trail, and if that happens you get out of the way quick. They're like a giant bowling ball then, and the weight of their bottoms is enough to crush anyone in their path.'

Barnabus makes a mental note never to get crushed by a gleewatt's bottom.

'Where do they come from?' he asks.

His aunt shrugs. 'No-one knows. They've been here

as long as the Clockwork. Ah! Here comes Brixton. I was hoping we'd be able to hitch a lift.'

A short, rotund man comes strolling towards them with a long-handled paddle resting on his shoulder.

'Alright, Jem,' he says. 'Heading for home?'

'If it's not out of your way,' Aunt Jemima replies.

'Not at all. Been shovelling nuggets all morning. Time for some nice, clean paperwork. Car's this way.'

'Appreciate it, Brixton, thanks.'

As they follow the man's lead, Barnabus whispers to his aunt, 'What did he mean, shovelling nuggets?'

'Nuggets of poop. Moth poop. He's been clearing it up, shovelling it into piles.'

'Ew.'

'Well, the gleewatts have to eat.'

'What? They eat *poop*? That's disgusting!'

'Not if you're a gleewatt.'

CHAPTER EIGHT

THE SWAYING HOUSE

Barnabus has to stifle a giggle when he sees Brixton's car. It reminds Barnabus of a toy car that Aunt Gladys once gave him on his birthday. (She took the toy away two days later, as punishment, when he suggested donating money to the children's ward of the local hospital.)

Brixton's car is about half the size of a real car and has no roof. It is red, with chunky tyres and a round, bubble-like body that wouldn't look strange with a big smiley face painted on the bonnet. But what makes it seem most toy-like is the large metal key that sticks out on one side.

'Just gotta wind it up,' Brixton says, grabbing the key and turning it. 'Won't take a minute.'

Aunt Jemima climbs into the passenger seat in front, not bothering to open the door, and Barnabus climbs into the seat behind her. When Brixton is done winding the key, he gets into the driver's seat and grins back at Barnabus.

'All set? Hold on tight now, it goes a fair pace when it's fully wound up and the brake comes off.'

Barnabus grips the door handle and the car takes off at terrific speed with a loud *whiiiizzzzzzzzzzzz*.

'It's the last of the red cars left after we'd a bunch stolen,' Brixton shouts to Aunt Jemima over the noise. 'Did you know?'

'No!' she yells back. 'Is it that bad?'

'Gotta good few blue cars still. And the yellows aren't doing too bad. But the greens and purples are dwindling now as well. Winders just can't keep up with the repairs.'

Aunt Jemima shakes her head. 'Have you no good news for me, Brixton?'

'You stepped in moth poop back there,' he replies. 'That's meant to bring good luck.'

The woman lifts her foot and sniffs. 'Oh, for heaven's sake!'

They race along the pathways, which Brixton seems to know like the back of his hand. With no barriers on the wooden paths, there are moments when Barnabus is sure they must go shooting off the trail and into the Clockwork gears, but they never do. He finally relaxes into the thrill of the ride, leaning his head out to enjoy the rush of air that blasts through his hair. Had Barnabus ever been allowed to have a dog, and had that dog ever been allowed in one of the Kwerks' limousines with the windows open, it might have done exactly the same thing.

Aunt Jemima calmly points out golden pieces as they zoom along – fierce-looking escape wheels with curving teeth; heavy balance wheels that swing back and forth, back and forth, almost as hypnotic as the springing gleewatts; levers with bobbing heads that trigger the striking trains.

'The bells are struck at regular intervals,' Aunt Jemima says, 'so we can tell which sections need tuning up and which sections are running … well, like clockwork.'

'I like the chiming,' Barnabus says, listening for the strike of the bells. 'It's a lovely sound.'

'Isn't it? Literal music to my ears.'

They fly through healthy golden areas and gloomy sick ones, the car spiralling up the circling pathway of another Weight Station, dodging the galloping glee-watts. Huge, feathery frilly moths soar over from time to time, and twice they pass other cars (which are heart-stopping moments, given that the wooden path is barely wide enough for two). Barnabus hardly dares to blink. He doesn't want to miss a moment of this incredible new world.

Eventually the red car begins to slow, and the whiz-zing sound of its wind-up engine gets lower and lower.

'Coming up on your stop, Jem,' Brixton says.

He gently pulls the brake and the car buzzes to a halt next to a rickety wooden house suspended by many ropes, which sways noticeably.

Aunt Jemima leaps from the car. 'Cheers for the lift, Brixton.'

The man waves in reply, getting out to wind the key once more, and Barnabus follows his aunt to the door of the swaying house.

'Mind the gap,' Aunt Jemima says, pulling the door open and stepping inside from the path.

It's not that big a gap, but the slight swinging of both the path and the house make Barnabus a little nervous – he takes the biggest step he can over the threshold.

Inside, his aunt lifts the delicate glass shade of an oil lamp and lights the wick. She replaces the shade, and a warm glow fills the hallway.

'No lamps lit means there's nobody home,' she says.

At that moment, a pale, wiry arm snakes from a tall cupboard nearby and smacks its hand on the door. Barnabus nearly falls to the floor in fright.

'My apologies,' Aunt Jemima says, seemingly embarrassed. 'There's always *one* person at home. But when the lamps aren't lit, it means everyone else is out. We've got a quiet house for the time being.'

Apparently appeased, the arm slides back into the cupboard and the door is pulled tightly shut.

'Who …' Barnabus asks. 'Who was that?'

'That's just the cupboard,' Aunt Jemima replies. 'She makes trouble when she can, but otherwise you can ignore her.'

Barnabus's eyes are wide.

'She never comes out,' his aunt assures him. 'Come on, kitchen's upstairs. I think we could both do with a sandwich and a nice cup of tea.'

Barnabus watches the brimming teacup in front of him and wonders if any liquid will spill over the sides. Staring at the cup is not helping his seasickness. The house moves like a sailboat on the calmest of oceans, but Barnabus has never been to sea (or anywhere else for that matter), so he has had no practice sitting still while the vessel around him is in motion. Even car rides in one of the family's limousines only ever took him the length of the Big House's driveway. He wants to enjoy his first visit to another house and the tea might help settle his stomach, but he can't quite bring himself to drink it.

The smell of his aunt is not helping. The just-poured-tar scent has returned like a thick plume of smoke. Barnabus pinches his nostrils to block it out, but he can't keep hold of his nose forever.

'Smell something bad?' his aunt asks.

Barnabus blushes. The woman smiles at him from across the table, sipping her own tea and chewing on a cucumber sandwich.

Barnabus shakes his head and takes a quick gulp of tea, dribbling some down his chin. His aunt holds out the plate of sandwiches and as he leans in to take one, she says, 'Is it a burnt smell? Rubbery. Like someone's pouring a new road.'

He freezes. Feeling rude, he nods.

Aunt Jemima doesn't seem offended. She grins.

'I thought so,' she says. 'I thought I caught you sniffing in the Big House this morning, every time I tried to get close. You couldn't see me cos of those revolting Kwerks – ugh, like a wall made of drain hair and the gunk that goes with it. But you could smell me.'

Barnabus isn't sure what to say. 'Is it perfume?' he asks.

His aunt laughs out loud. 'Might as well be! It is the most glorious scent in the world. I wish very much that I could smell it.'

'You can't?'

'Not even a little bit.'

'But it's very strong. Much stronger now than it was this morning. It's almost …'

'Overpowering?'

'Yes,' Barnabus says with an apologetic look. He doesn't want to hurt his aunt's feelings.

She pulls a balled-up handkerchief from her pocket and places it on the table. 'Can you tell me what's inside?' she asks.

Barnabus shakes his head. His aunt pushes the hand-kerchief closer.

'Try.'

The hot-tar scent is all around, but there's also a delicate thread of it wafting from the balled-up fabric.

'The smell is coming from there,' he says. 'But it's everywhere as well.'

Still smiling, Aunt Jemima unwraps the handkerchief to reveal a small nugget of gold. 'There was a time,' she says, 'when every single Kwerk could smell gold. It was a great gift, and our ancestors used it to sniff out the purest gold to help repair and rebuild broken parts of the Clockwork. The Kwerk family helped to keep the world turning … once upon a time.'

Barnabus gazes at the nugget on the table. It doesn't make sense – that he can smell something metal – but as soon as his aunt says it, he knows it is true. He can smell the gold like it's newly steamrolled tarmac. He can smell every dent and scratch of the misshapen piece.

He can smell the Clockwork too, he realises. The explosion of scent on entering the golden moon wasn't his aunt at all, but the powerful rush of hot tar from all that glorious, gorgeous gold.

'I don't understand,' he says. 'If every Kwerk can smell it, why can't you?'

Aunt Jemima sits back in her chair. 'The ability died out generations ago. Great-Aunt Claudia was the last of our family to have it, and hers was very weak. She used to wear diamond plugs up her nostrils to remind everyone of her gift.'

Barnabus nods. 'Uncle Horace said they protected her precious sense of smell.'

'As if she needed them.' Aunt Jemima rolls her eyes. 'Great-Aunt Claudia could barely smell gold when it was close enough to tickle her nose hairs.'

Reaching out to touch the little nugget in the handkerchief, Barnabus asks, 'How come I can smell it then?'

'Well,' his aunt replies, 'the story goes that when the Kwerks' gift began to shrink, their greed began to grow. Perhaps it was the other way around – as they got greedier, their gift got weaker.'

'And now?' says Barnabus.

'And now?' Aunt Jemima shrugs. 'Your mother and I were a non-greedy blip in the Kwerk dynasty. You make it more of a pattern. Perhaps there's a new line of Kwerks emerging – a branch shooting off that dreadful family tree. Perhaps the next generation will all have the gift. Perhaps you're just the first.'

CHAPTER NINE

HANGING OFF A WHEEL

'Is this why you brought me here?' Barnabus asks. 'To sniff out gold for you. For the Clockwork, I mean.'

'Oh no, little plum,' Aunt Jemima replies. 'I'm delighted that you have the gift, but whether you use it or not is a question for when you're grown. A happy life is all I want for you. So school first, big life decisions later.'

'But if I'm the first in the family to have the gift in a long time, maybe I'm supposed to start now. Maybe it's fate.'

'Maybe it is,' his aunt says, 'if you believe in that kind of thing. But while you're in my charge you'll have every opportunity made available to you. And that means not locking you into a lifelong career when you're only knee high to a short chicken. Now, get some sandwiches into you before your tummy starts growling.'

Barnabus bites into a sandwich, suddenly realising how hungry he is. Breakfast was a long time ago. He smiles at the thought. At the breakfast table he was surrounded by awful Kwerks in foul moods, sniping at each other. Now look where he is. What a weird and wonderful day this has turned out to be.

All at once the swaying house lurches. There is noise on the ground floor, and someone comes thundering up the stairs. Then there's banging and slamming in the hall outside the kitchen.

'Samson, is that you?' Aunt Jemima calls out. 'You've made me spill my tea.'

A large man stumbles into the kitchen in a tangle of ropes, carrying weights and clamps in his huge hands.

'Jem,' he cries, 'Abigail's fallen! She's hanging off a wheel. She saved a moth-watcher from toppling off the path, and now she's, she's—'

He leans over, gasping for breath.

'Couple of deep breaths, Sammy,' Aunt Jemima says, springing to her feet and deftly unknotting the ropes in which he's tangled. 'If anyone can survive a fall through the gears, it's Abigail. The girl's unrufflable.'

She vanishes into the hall and returns with what appears to be a large, folded tarpaulin.

'The car outside?' she asks, and the large man nods. 'Right, let's get the gear in, chop, chop. Barnabus, you can stay or come with us. If you're coming with us, you need to move your feet.'

Eager to be part of the team, Barnabus jumps out of his seat and follows them to a yellow car parked in front of the house. He climbs in the back and Aunt Jemima dumps the gear next to him while Samson winds the car's key.

Aunt Jemima drives this time, and she is fiendishly quick behind the wheel. Samson is not the best at giving directions – 'It's right here. No, no, I mean left! No wait, right!' – but the woman responds with lightning reflexes, and before long Samson is shouting,

'There! There she is! Still on the wheel, thank goodness.'

They are approaching the two moth-watchers who'd been in the Botanical Gardens earlier that day. Only Francis has the grace to look bashful. Maura is defiant.

'It's not our fault!' she yells with her camera in her hands. 'I'd've got the shot if the silly girl hadn't pushed me back onto the path. Purple-feathered juvenile, perfect specimen. If she hadn't …'

Her voice fades as the car speeds past, leaving her behind.

'Moth-watchers,' Aunt Jemima growls. 'They're a bloody menace.'

'Abigail's back there,' Samson cries over the whizz of the engine.

'I saw her,' Aunt Jemima replies. 'But we'll not get her from here. We need to get underneath her.'

Barnabus turns to look. He didn't see any girl.

The car spirals down the wooden trails, tilting on two wheels as it takes a sharp corner. Soon Barnabus can see the moth-watchers again, staring down from a trail high above the car at a figure dangling from a turning golden wheel. Barnabus's breath catches in his throat.

'There she is!' Samson is kneeling on the passenger seat, pointing vigorously. 'There she is!'

'I see her,' Aunt Jemima responds. 'Sit back down or we'll lose you too.'

The car skids to a halt underneath the dangling figure, but she is so far above them Barnabus can't imagine how Aunt Jemima plans to save her.

From what Barnabus can see, the girl is remarkably calm. She is wearing a blue boiler suit and appears to be caught on a cog of the wheel by her collar. As the wheel rotates to the bottom, she simply reaches up a hand to hold on so she doesn't slip off.

'You alright, Abigail?' Aunt Jemima yells.

'All good,' the girl yells back. 'But on my last rotation, I think. My collar's about to give.'

Aunt Jemima leans over Barnabus to grab the pile of tarpaulin which she throws onto the boards, slamming her foot on an automatic pump that Barnabus didn't know was there. The pile of fabric immediately begins to inflate.

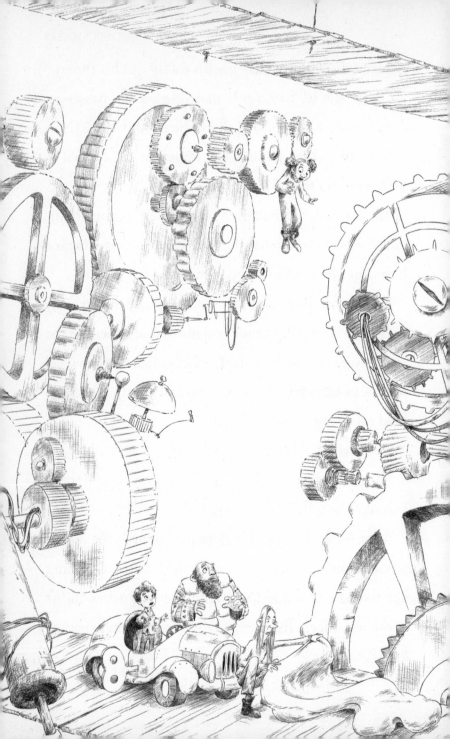

'Twenty seconds,' Aunt Jemima shouts.

'It'll be close,' the girl replies.

She isn't kidding. Barnabus holds tight to the driver's seat in front, gawping between the too-slowly-inflating tarpaulin mattress and the too-fast-moving golden wheel. The girl's body jerks as her collar tears further, then there's one more rip and she is falling. Barnabus stands up as if he can catch her as she sails down, down, down.

WHUFF.

Abigail hits the tarpaulin just as it reaches full inflation. She vanishes into the bobbing mattress until Aunt Jemima digs her out and helps her onto the wooden boards.

'You alright?' the woman asks.

'Yeah, yeah, I'm good. I wasn't wheely worried.' The girl smiles widely. 'I wasn't *wheely* worried. Like, *really* worried.'

'Please get in the car.'

'Alright.'

While Samson grills Abigail to make sure she's not

injured, Aunt Jemima deflates the massive mattress and climbs back into the driver's seat. Abigail is squashed between Barnabus and the gear. She is a few years older than him, with large, lively eyes.

'Hello,' she says, and Barnabus blushes.

'Hi.'

'This is my nephew,' Aunt Jemima says as Samson winds the car. 'Barnabus. He's new to the Clockwork.'

'Hello, Barnabus,' Abigail says, and he blushes again.

The girl doesn't seem any the worse for her very recent brush with death. Barnabus can't fathom it.

Samson climbs back into the passenger seat, and Aunt Jemima releases the brake. Abigail immediately pulls an object from her pocket that looks like the bell of a small trumpet and puts the narrow end of the tube in her ear.

'The car's mainspring needs greasing, Jem,' she says.

Aunt Jemima shakes her head. 'If you ever did fall to your death, Abigail, do you think you'd notice? Or would you just keep working?'

'Keep working, probably.'

'It was me who took the car out, Abigail,' Samson says. 'I'll let Brixton know about the mainspring.'

Barnabus is looking at the little trumpet device with interest, and Abigail smiles. 'It's an ear horn,' she explains. 'Electronic stuff doesn't tend to work very well down here, so we stick to the basics. You can hear echoes of kinks in the Clockwork from miles away with an ear horn. With a bit of practice, that is. Wanna try?'

Barnabus puts the horn to his ear and frowns. All he can hear is a cacophony of clanging, ticking and chiming. Abigail laughs at his expression.

'With practice,' she repeats.

'Right,' Aunt Jemima says, taking a sharp turn in the path. 'Back home we go.'

'Nope,' Abigail says. 'The Doom Room, please. I have a couple of things I'd like to run by Morfidius.'

'Ugh,' Aunt Jemima replies. 'It's been a long day already. I can do without the gloom of the Doom Room.'

'I'm happy to take the car if you'd like to walk back to the house,' says Abigail.

Aunt Jemima scowls in reply.

'Oh,' says Samson, 'and if you could drop me off in Sector J on the way, that would be great.'

'Oh sure,' Aunt Jemima snaps. 'I'll just be everybody's chauffeur. Anywhere you'd like to go, Barnabus, while we're at it?'

She means it sarcastically, but Barnabus is tempted to say 'back to the house'. He wants to know what the Doom Room is. He wants to know what's in Sector J. But this day has been ridiculous. Wonderful and awe-inspiring and heart-stoppingly exciting. But ridiculous. He is exhausted. He longs for a nap.

As the others relax into conversation, Barnabus rests his head against the door of the car and lets the droning sound of the wind-up engine soothe him into sleep.

CHAPTER TEN

HISTORY AND SCIENCE AND ALL THAT

Barnabus wakes with a start. He is alone in the car and it's dark all around.

'Aunt Jemima?'

There is no reply.

The car is parked in a sick area of the Clockwork. In fact, this is the sickest part that Barnabus has seen so far. The oily, blackened wheels don't turn at all, they are still. There is the distant sound of ticking and chiming from some healthier place, but it sounds muffled and very far away.

'Aunt Jemima?'

Barnabus gets out of the car, but the oil lamps directly overhead are barely glowing and he dares not go too far without proper light. He could walk right off the path.

'Are you lost?' says a voice suddenly in the darkness.

Barnabus jumps. 'Who's there?'

He hears sliding footsteps on the wooden boards, as though someone doesn't care to lift their feet as they walk.

'I'm Greeg,' the voice replies. 'I can help you find your way if you're lost.'

'No, thank you.' Barnabus's own voice is trembling. 'I'm just waiting for my aunt. She won't be long.'

'Oh, she'll be ages. Things move very slowly in the Doom Room.'

Barnabus's eyes are adjusting to the dimness, and he can see the outline of the creature. It looks like a very large hedgehog, prickly all over with short legs and bright-blue eyes that shine in the dark.

'Oh, she really won't be long,' Barnabus says, trying not to sound anxious. 'She told me to wait by the car.'

'Hmm. Well, in that case, perhaps you can help *me*,'

Greeg says. 'I'm looking for my whurl. Have you seen her?'

'For your what?'

'My whurl. My pet. My transport. She's about so big, has seven furry tentacles and adorable little fangs. Just an average-looking whurl. You haven't seen her?'

'Em, no. I'm afraid not.'

'Oh dear. Well, do keep an eye out. Her name is Blink, and she's ever so friendly. Loves to spring out of nowhere and grab onto strangers. For hugs, I mean. Her tentacles are terribly ticklish.'

'Oh. She sounds lovely.' Barnabus nervously glances around. If a furry, tentacled creature with fangs leaps on him out of nowhere, he thinks he might scream. 'If I see her, I'll … I'll let you know.'

Greeg nods. 'How kind. It was nice to meet you, Barnabus.'

'It was nice to meet you …' Barnabus trails off, realising that he never told the creature his name.

'Bye for now,' says the prickly hedgehog, and he is quickly lost in the gloom.

* * *

If you found this encounter a little unnerving, then please rest assured that Barnabus does find Aunt Jemima shortly afterwards and is introduced to the wonders of the Doom Room. And if you're worried that the Doom Room sounds a little scary, then you can put your mind at ease. Because it wasn't always called the Doom Room. It was once called the Float-About-a-Boat Room, and it was a bustling, bright and fun place to be. The nickname 'Doom Room' came along some time after the Clockwork began to get sick. The following is a short lesson in history and/or science:

There was a time, many generations ago, when the Clockwork was a well-known and much-visited part of the planet. Everyone knew the basics of how the world turned and how essential to its survival was its glorious, golden centre. And far from the quiet, almost personless place it is today, the Clockwork was once extraordinarily busy. Winders (those that carry out repairs on the precious works) were too many to count.

You couldn't swing a cat without hitting a smelter (someone who melts and moulds new gold pieces). Bridge-thinkers were two a penny (we'd probably call them architects today) and bridge-builders were as common as daisies in a field (and would likely be known as engineers now). The Clockwork was also overrun with scientists of every kind, studying things like the elasticity of air, the smudginess of light, and the viscosity of sound. Their research was done for the benefit of the Earth, for the benefit of humankind, and for the pursuit of knowledge itself.

Beastie-brutey-fiendy-finders (biffs for short, or what we'd call zoologists) and veggie-viney-weedy-zeals (also called veez, but these days we'd probably say botanists) had plenty to keep themselves occupied in studying the strange and fascinating animal and plant life at the heart of the planet. The slurping slug, for example, could provide several lifetimes' worth of research opportunities; its slippery slime alone was studied by over a hundred scientists due to its wonderful moisturising qualities. The clanging beetle

WINDER

BEASTIE-BRUTEY-
FIENDY-FINDERS
(BIFFS)

VEGGIE-VINEY-
WEEDY-ZEAL (VEEZ)

SMELTER

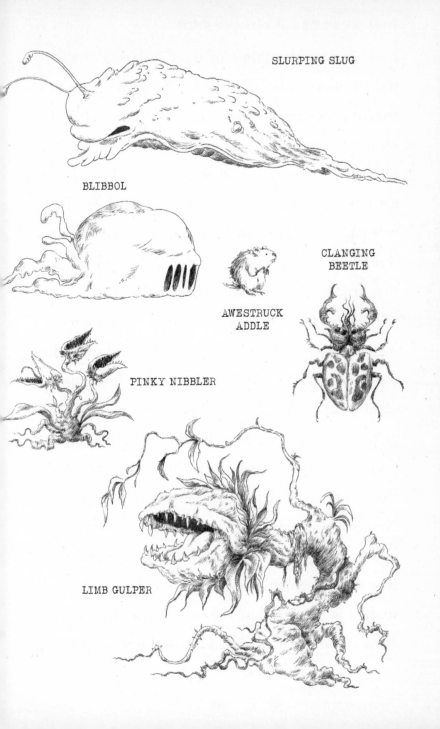

SLURPING SLUG

BLIBBOL

AWESTRUCK
ADDLE

CLANGING
BEETLE

PINKY NIBBLER

LIMB GULPER

could imitate the chime of the Clockwork's bells so well, it often fooled winders and bridge-builders into thinking they were behind schedule. Rubbery blibbols moved through the gears by plopping from tooth to tooth like blobs of goo, though they had no trouble catching their tiny prey – the awestruck addles. These vole-like creatures were easily mesmerised by shiny things, which was a very unfortunate trait for animals that lived in an environment made of gold.

The plant life of the Clockwork was equally interesting and sometimes even more dangerous to study. The carnivorous pinky nibbler might only nip at the toe of an unlucky passerby, whereas the much bigger limb gulper could grab a considerably larger piece. (This magnificent giant was a rare plant back in the Clockwork's heyday and is suspected to be extinct now.) Numerous species of crawling moss used to cover houses at the centre of the world like patchwork quilts; they went creeping over pathways and up walls when studied in the wild, and the ones in the lab tended to sneak out of their specimen jars and into lunchboxes.

Many a scientist cried out in horror on unwrapping their sandwich to find what looked like dreadfully mouldy bread.

As you can probably imagine, the structures, pathways and homes of the Clockwork were much more elaborate and secure in those days than the simple, swaying paths that exist now. It was a glorious wooden metropolis, where people lived and worked in wonderful harmony, much like a finely tuned clock. And at the centre of all of this was a splendidly strange area of lightness; lightness in the very literal sense. In the globe-shaped space at the heart of the Clockwork, you float. Much like you would in outer space. Except that in outer space, you float because there is no gravity; at the centre of the Clockwork, you float because there is *too much* gravity.

You might already know this, but gravity is an invisible force that pulls you and everything else in the world towards the ground. It's why things fall down and not up. And no matter where you are on Earth, that doesn't change. Things in Greenland fall down.

And, at the opposite side of the planet, things in Australia also fall down. It's as if gravity wants everything to move towards the most central point of the planet. So when you're actually *in* the most central point of the planet, gravity is pulling from all directions in equal measure. So instead of falling down (or up), you do neither. You kind of hang in the middle. And it's lovely. Because you're floating. Like a helium-filled balloon.

This floaty space became the hub where people got together to talk about what was going on in the Clockwork and to make decisions about things. They picked it because it was the very centre of the Clockwork – the heart of it – but also because it was great fun. People could float freely there, or they could strap into one of the many wooden boats that drifted through the space. (Boats were preferable for those who wanted to write things down or have smaller meetings with just two or three people, rather than yelling at each other across lots of floating bodies.)

When it came to giving this area a name, there were many very sensible suggestions: The Meeting

Space, The Central Hub, The Societal and Govern-mental Congregational Area for the Dissemination of Information. But one Clockwork resident argued that Float-About-a-Boat Room was not only descriptive, it was also entertaining. The Central Hub, for example, was not fun to say ten times fast. Float-About-a-Boat Room was. The resident demonstrated this by saying the name ten times fast, which ended up sounding like 'Fluttery Butt Room', and everyone laughed. The name immediately stuck, since the people of the Clockwork understood that important and sensible things should also be entertaining whenever possible.

Currently, the Float-About-a-Boat Room exists in much the same state as it did in better days, except that it's almost entirely empty. Without gold-sniffers, there is no steady supply of good-quality gold to repair and replace faulty or stolen Clockwork pieces. Replace-ment gears of brass, iron and steel don't last long, and they damage the valuable pieces around them, which are in turn replaced by inferior wheels, and so the sickness spreads.

The Clockwork was once a bustling wooden metropolis, jammed with swaying houses, offices, workshops, laboratories, cafés, restaurants and the occasional pub. But as the gears got sicker and the work got harder, the golden moon became a less joyful place in which to live. People chose to move on, and no newcomers arrived to replace those who left. Empty wooden buildings became derelict and eventually fell apart, leaving only sparse trails and the few swaying houses that exist today. So, with just a small number of people left in the Clockwork, there aren't many to occupy its gravity-filled heart at any one time. And ever since the golden workings began to get sick, and the information shared in the Float-About-a-Boat Room became inevitably gloomy, the space adopted the name Doom Room instead. It's a sad label for an otherwise wonderful place, but there we are.

You may be feeling a bit glum now and filled to the brim with historical and scientific knowledge, so let's take a little break before we rejoin Barnabus in the next chapter.

CHAPTER ELEVEN

THE DOOM ROOM

If you remember, Barnabus is at this moment standing alone near the car, wondering where on earth his aunt has got to. He knows that she and Abigail were heading to a place called the Doom Room, but he can't see a door or a passage or anything else that might lead to a room. There's just the sick Clockwork all around and the wooden pathways that zigzag through it.

He is half thinking of winding up the car and driving in search of Aunt Jemima (and the thought of climbing behind the wheel and whizzing off at top speed is already making him smile) when he hears a strange sound. It's not the sliding footsteps of the prickly Greeg (which Barnabus is very glad about), but a kind of squeaky chomping, as though something metal is eating something else metal.

He searches for what's causing the sound, and a shiver runs down his spine when he spots a fluffy (or possibly furry) thing sitting on one of the frozen, blackened gears, apparently chewing on the metal.

A whurl.

Barnabus gasps loudly at the thought, which appears to startle the creature. It springs from the gear, throwing its furry tentacles wide, and Barnabus falls backwards.

Did you ever get such a fright that everything seems to happen in slow motion? Barnabus has that very experience right now. Falling backwards should only take an instant, and yet he has plenty of time to realise what's going on.

He notices that the creature's dreadfully long tentacles are more feathery than furry, and it doesn't appear to have fangs of any kind. A split second later and it's clear that the tentacles are in fact wings, and that the animal is a frilly moth, not a whurl.

It's amazing that the human mind can work so quickly in these situations, but it is baffling that this remarkable ability is often of no use whatsoever. Because although Barnabus has now correctly identified the animal that gave him such a fright, and has correctly surmised that the moth is of no danger to him, and has also realised that he has no need to fall backwards to avoid it, Barnabus is still falling backwards. And with the continued irony of the fast-moving human mind and the slow-moving human body, he realises one more thing: he was at the edge of the path when he began to fall.

The dark, oily wheels above him are zipping away as he plunges through the wheels below, and there is nothing he can do to save himself. More than frightened, he feels terribly sad. This is his very first day being free of the Kwerks and the Big House, and already the adventure is over. And what an adventure it has been! Barnabus has seen things he could never have imagined and learned more about the world than he would have thought possible. In the days that follow he would surely have learned so much more and seen so many more incredible, beautiful, awe-inspiring things. But it is not to be. Barnabus closes his eyes and tries to feel grateful for the day he has had.

'You're awake. Marvellous.'

Barnabus opens his eyes and sees Aunt Jemima looking down at him. Oddly, her long curtain of black hair stands out from her head in thick strands, like spider legs. What's even stranger is that he can see her feet. And Abigail's feet. But Abigail is above his aunt and Barnabus can see the *soles* of her shoes ... He can't figure out what's what or who's where.

'Am I ... dead?' he asks.

His aunt frowns. 'I certainly hope not. Why don't you hitch a lift on a boat there? The Doom Room can be a little disorienting on your first visit.'

Barnabus's first impression of the Doom Room is that it's not a room at all. He can still see the Clockwork and the gears he fell through. He is in a gap in the workings – a ball of space inside the mass of wheels. And he must have landed on the softest of pillows because he can't feel what's underneath him. He turns to check and suffers another fright. There is nothing underneath him. Just more space, and below that, more Clockwork.

'How is it … How am I …?'

'Oh yes, yes,' his aunt says. 'Delightful little quirk of physics in this spot – you float. Don't worry, you'll get used to it. But do get yourself into a boat for the time being. Newcomers left to drift in the Doom Room tend to lose their lunch.'

Barnabus is starting to feel a little queasy. Since breakfast there's been a swooping hang glider ride, a curling squidgy bit tunnel, swinging pathways, whizzing cars, a swaying house, a near fall from the path, an *actual* fall from the path, and now a floating-in-the-air. His tummy isn't terribly happy.

He sees one of the wooden boats his aunt is talking about – it's floating past as if on calm waters – and grabs onto the side. About to roll into it, he nearly jumps out of his skin when a shrivelled face emerges from the boat and shrieks, 'This one's taken!'

'Meant to say,' Aunt Jemima calls out, 'watch out for the old ones. They can be a bit crabby.'

'*Old* ones?' comes a bark from another boat. 'You watch your manners, missy, or you'll be out on your ear!'

'My apologies, Elvira. I meant the older residents of the Doom Room.'

'Of the *Central Hub*,' the barker in the boat snaps. 'Doom Room. Ridiculous name. As bad as Float-About-a-Boat.'

The old woman continues to gripe, but her voice is lost to Barnabus as her wooden vessel moves across the space. He finds an empty boat and gets in, locating a belt that clips around his waist, holding him in place. Finally able to relax, he pauses to properly take in his surroundings. Aunt Jemima and Abigail are drifting freely in the air, and both appear to be comfortable despite the fact that they are very slowly turning in opposite directions. They continue to chat and nod, though they're rarely face to face. They're talking to an older man – not quite as old as the boat-based residents appear to be, but very old nonetheless. He is extremely tall, loose-limbed and loose-spined, never straight, constantly in a delicate, snake-like motion. He seems able to direct his movement through the space with the smallest of gestures – a raised eyebrow and he drifts gently upwards, a waggling finger and he floats to the left. However, he doesn't seem bothered by Aunt Jemima and Abigail's less controlled movements. He follows them easily as they drift and turn, and their talking is never interrupted by all the motion. They appear to be discussing the state of the Clockwork, though Barnabus only catches snippets as he and they float apart.

'*Psst.*'

Barnabus looks up at a boat that is drifting above him. It's upside down – or is his own boat upside down? Either way, he and the old man inside can see each other.

'*Psst,*' the man says again. 'Are you new?'

'I … yes, I suppose so. This is my first time in the Clockwork.'

'Then I hope you won't ignore your elders. Like them others.'

'Too bloody right,' says another voice from below. The woman stretches up to tap on the hull of Barnabus's boat. 'Wisdom comes with age. But do they ever ask us what we think?'

'Only interested in what Morfidius has to say,' says yet another occupant of a nearby boat. Barnabus seems surrounded by them now.

'Morfidius?' Barnabus asks.

'My great-grandnephew,' someone replies, pointing to the man talking with Aunt Jemima and Abigail.

'Just grandnephew to me,' says another.

'Bright enough for a whippersnapper, but he's not got *all* the answers.'

'Isn't that the truth? There's plenty of Grandthumbs around here with good advice to give. How come it's only Morfidius Grandthumb they ask?'

'Ageism.'

'You're right.'

'Don't know what they're missing.'

'Like what?' Barnabus interrupts. 'What advice are they missing out on?'

The floating boat occupants seem surprised by the question.

'Well ...' says the upside-down man who initially spoke. 'Well ... for one thing, you should pay attention to what you hear.'

'To *everything* you hear,' another agrees.

'You hear whispers of things, you don't ignore them,' says the woman from below. 'We all knew that when *we* were on the job.'

Someone else nods. 'The young ones don't know that. Think it's all just noise. They don't pay attention.'

All the older people are nodding now, and Barnabus smiles politely. He understands why their advice might not be considered particularly helpful.

'I'll remember that,' he says, to be nice.

The boat occupants seem pleased.

'You come back any time, my dear boy,' says the upside-down man as he floats away.

'Any time,' the woman below says. 'Refreshing to

meet someone with an open mind. Finally.'

'Mmhmm.'

'Yes, *finally*.'

Barnabus drifts beyond the huddle of boats and sits back to wait for Aunt Jemima.

CHAPTER TWELVE

AROUND THE TABLE

'I don't suppose you grabbed a bellows on the way down?' Aunt Jemima asks.

Still strapped into the boat, Barnabus shakes his head. 'What for?'

'For getting out of the Doom Room.' She removes a pair of wooden bellows that she has slung over her shoulder, the kind that might have been used to stoke a fire many years ago. 'No worries, I'll give you a piggyback. On you get.'

Barnabus climbs out of the boat carefully, so as not to send himself floating away, and grabs onto his aunt's back.

'Hold on tight now,' she says, pulling open the accordion-like instrument so it sucks in air, then squeezing it closed.

Air wheezes from the nozzle, pushing Barnabus and Aunt Jemima backwards. She does it again, and again, and again. The breeze from the bellows ruffles the hair of a man in a boat nearby.

'Oi!' he shrieks. 'Watch where you're blowing!'

'Sorry, Fagan,' Aunt Jemima replies.

Barnabus is enjoying the bellows ride. His aunt is strong and good at directing the flow of air. They zip across the Doom Room in a way that reminds him of a pinched balloon suddenly let go, though not quite as fast.

He glances behind and sees Abigail bellowing her way towards a rope ladder in the same manner. She throws the bellows over her shoulder and climbs the ladder just ahead of Barnabus and his aunt.

'Careful now,' Aunt Jemima tells him. 'When we reach regular gravity, you're going to feel as heavy as a gleewatt's bottom.'

She's right. Barnabus doesn't usually feel like a bag full of anvils, but with every metre they travel he feels heavier and heavier. Holding on gets more difficult. He is beginning to slide off his aunt's back.

'Aunt Jemima!'

'Nearly there.' Her voice is reassuring. 'Aaaand we're on.'

They are safe on one of the wooden trails. Barnabus slips to the boards, feeling very much like a gleewatt's bottom, while Aunt Jemima and Abigail hang their bellows on a rack with dozens of others.

'Well, I don't know about you two,' says Aunt Jemima, 'but I'm so hungry I could eat a walrus that's eaten a horse that's eaten a goose. Time for dinner.'

The kitchen table in the swaying house is rattling. Barnabus is slowly becoming used to the sailboat feeling of being in the house, but Samson's raucous laughter is making the table shake even more.

'And then he reaches up with the paddle to dislodge the moth and – *plop* – the rotten creature poops all over him!' Samson wipes a tear from his eye. 'I swear, I laughed so hard I nearly tumbled off the path.'

Aunt Jemima and Abigail are laughing loudly. Barnabus is too. He is so happy. When, from his attic window, he would watch the children of Undle being collected from school, this is what he imagined they were going home to. Dinner in the kitchen with all their family, telling them about their day, talking and laughing and talking some more. Barnabus was always so envious. He longed for moments like that. And now he is living them.

Samson made a huge pot of delicious stew that sits in the middle of the table next to a plate of warm rolls for mopping up the scrumptious sauce. It's the best thing Barnabus has ever tasted.

'So, Barnabus,' Samson says, 'tell us about your day. Was it a big adventure getting here from ... where was it?'

'Undle,' Aunt Jemima says.

'Oh yeah, that's right. Undle. Was it a long trip?'

'Yes,' Barnabus replies. 'Although, I've never really been anywhere before, so next door would have been a long trip for me.'

That gets everyone laughing again, and Barnabus is delighted. He tells Samson and Abigail all about Great-Aunt Claudia's funeral, about the hang glider flight and the Botanical Gardens and the moth-watchers and the helicopter and the squidgy bit. He tells them about the long walk to the Clockwork, his first sight of the golden gears, the fright he got from a frilly moth, and how he watched the happy gleewatts catapulting across the Weight Station. And as he talks, he can't believe he's talking about himself. This is an adventure *he* has had; Barnabus Kwerk, the little boy who never left his attic room.

'And then I woke up in the car, and there was this prickly animal that said hello to me and–'

'Wait, what?' Aunt Jemima says. 'What prickly animal?'

'I don't know what he was, but he said his name was

Greeg and he was looking for his, em … his pet or something.'

'Whurl,' Abigail says, her voice low. 'Greeg is a crug.'

'Crugs and whurls go together like sauerkraut and pickled fish,' says Samson.

'Is that all he said?' Aunt Jemima asks.

'Yes,' says Barnabus. 'And then he left. And then I got a fright because I thought I saw the … whurl, but it was just a moth. That's how I fell off the path into the Doom Room.'

'Crugs and whurls,' Aunt Jemima scowls. 'Dastardly beings. That was a very close call you had.'

'They run a black market with gold stolen from the Clockwork,' Abigail explains to Barnabus. 'And other terrible things. Basically, they're very bad news.'

Just then Barnabus remembers that the creature knew him by name, but he doesn't tell the others. Aunt Jemima seems so concerned that he's worried she might take him back to the surface. He goes on with his story instead, telling Samson about his first visit to the Doom Room.

'D'ya know,' the man says, 'when you hear it from an outsider's point of view, our life here sounds fantastical. Most days I think it's just shovelling poop and chasing off moths and fixing cars and inspecting gears. But it's a fabulous life really. I forget that sometimes. I'm glad to meet you, Barnabus. Glad you're here.'

He clinks glasses with him, and Barnabus smiles bashfully.

'I'll be doing a major repair in Sector F tomorrow,' Abigail says to him. 'There'll be abseiling and everything. You wanna help out?'

Barnabus lights up, but Aunt Jemima quickly interrupts before he can answer. 'Slow down, everybody. Don't go getting used to him. I brought Barnabus here so he could learn about his family history, but he'll be going back to the surface soon. To a normal life, with school and friends and normal things. When he's older he can decide whether or not he'd like to return to the Clockwork.'

'I *have* decided,' Barnabus says. 'I want to stay here. It's wonderful. And I can help, I can be useful. The sick parts have to be fixed, and since I can smell out the gold you need–'

Abigail's eyes nearly pop out of her head. 'You're a *gold-sniffer*?!'

Aunt Jemima stands suddenly with her hands held out. 'Enough!' she says. 'I get that this is all very exciting, but this is what's going to happen. Barnabus will return to the surface, and we'll get on with the usual works and repairs. If – and I mean *if* – he decides to return after he's graduated from school, or indeed from college, then he will be free to do so.'

Barnabus opens his mouth to object, but his aunt is having none of it.

'I heard you the first time,' she says. 'I get that you don't want to go back to the surface, but them's the berries. You're going. Besides, gold-sniffers didn't spend all their time in the Clockwork. They travelled the world searching for gold. You can't stay here forever *and* be a gold-sniffer.'

Barnabus hadn't thought of that. Still, he's sure he wants to be involved with the Clockwork in one way or another. It's too wonderful a thing to leave behind.

'Where are you gonna send the little tyke, Jem?' Samson asks.

'We'll have to decide that together, Barnabus and me,' the woman replies. 'But between all our friends on the surface there are plenty of places to choose from. You'll have your pick, Barnabus.'

'What about Widdlewell?' suggests Abigail.

Aunt Jemima sighs. 'That's too close to things. I want him apart from the Clockwork and everything to do with it, so he can see and experience different ways of living. So he can make informed decisions about his future. I won't force a life on him like Horace and the others would.'

Barnabus can't help feeling that Aunt Jemima is more like her brother than she'd care to admit. She says she won't force him into a particular life, but she won't let him choose the one he wants either.

'Right,' his aunt says, trying to clear away the bad mood by clearing the table. 'Time for bed, I think. We've all had a very long day.'

CHAPTER THIRTEEN

LOST WHISPERS

The house is quiet when Barnabus wakes. His eyes are still sticky with tiredness – he hasn't been asleep long.

He listens for Aunt Jemima or one of the others and hears nothing.

Odd. He's sure he heard someone whispering. Very close. It woke him up.

He sits up suddenly. There it is again. Definitely a whisper.

It sounds like it's coming from inside the bedroom, but in the delicate golden light reflected from the gears outside, he can't see anyone.

'Hello?' he says. 'Is someone there?'

There it is again, a soft, breathy sound, but muted.

Almost like it's coming from … inside the walls.

Barnabus presses his ear to the wall. There is a shushing sound inside there that ebbs and flows. For a split second he imagines he hears a word in the sound. Then he smiles to himself. All houses make noise. Barnabus knows this because the Big House makes more noise than most. A house that hangs on ropes and sways when someone steps through the front door must have plenty of its own sounds.

He lies down, and just before he drifts off to sleep, the words of the boat-floaters in the Doom Room come back to him: *Pay attention to* everything *you hear.*

Barnabus can't help it then. He listens harder to the shushing sounds inside the wall. Minutes later, he is convinced he is hearing words.

Downstairs, the whispers seem to say. *Downstairs, go, downstairs, in the hall.*

The whispers repeat and glide over each other, and it's hard to make them out.

Cupboard in the, downstairs, go, hall, go downstairs, in the hall, cupboard.

Curious, Barnabus whispers a question to the wall, but there is no answer. The same breathy words continue to repeat.

Barnabus goes to the door of his room and peeks out. Everyone else is in bed. He can hear snoring.

What harm could there be in doing what the whispers say, if he doesn't have to leave the house?

He tiptoes downstairs to the cupboard in the hall. It's taller than he remembers. The pale, wiry arm is out, resting on its cupboard door with fingers splayed. Barnabus gulps and clears his throat.

'Em, hello. I wonder if … I think I was told to come down here by, em …'

He's not sure what to say, and then the index finger of the pale arm stretches and curls. *Come here.*

Barnabus approaches slowly, and when he's very close,

SLAM.

The arm vanishes into the cupboard and the door shuts hard enough to sway the house.

The fright makes Barnabus feel weak, but also angry.

Aunt Jemima is right – this cupboard is a troublemaker.

He turns to go back upstairs when there's a *BANG* followed by another *SLAM*, and he spins to see a small trunk sitting on the hall floor. He thinks to knock on the cupboard door and deliver a few harsh words about scaring people in the middle of the night for no reason, but instead he pulls the trunk towards himself by the handle, staying out of grabbing distance should the pale arm reappear.

Lifting the lid of the trunk, he finds some dusty old books and a few grimy jars. He catches the word 'gold-sniffing' on one of the book covers.

'What are you doing up?'

Barnabus jumps. Aunt Jemima is staring sleepily at him from the bottom of the stairs.

'I …' he stammers. 'I was told to come down here.'

'Huh?'

Abigail calls from upstairs. 'What's the banging?'

'It's just the cupboard,' Aunt Jemima replies. 'Go back to sleep.'

The woman looks expectantly at Barnabus, and he

feels silly saying, 'Someone whispered at me to come downstairs. Whispered through the walls.'

Aunt Jemima's brow furrows for a moment, until the answer appears to dawn on her. 'Oh, a kind of shushing sound, was it? They're nothing. Whisps, we call them. They're just background noise you hear from time to time down here. Totally harmless.'

'It was words,' Barnabus says.

'Do you think so?' His aunt is smiling. 'You sound like Samson. Honestly, we hear them all the time. It's just the whining of the Clockwork echoing through the boards.'

'They told me to come downstairs.'

Aunt Jemima appears to ignore him. 'Samson calls them lost whispers. He thinks they're secrets that people have whispered into wood or stone. Like that old story, do you know the one? Where a boy whispers a secret to a tree, and when the tree is felled to make a harp, the harp sings the secret when played.'

She is still smiling, and Barnabus feels childish arguing any further.

'Can I take this back to my room?' he asks, pointing to the trunk.

'What's in it?'

'Books mostly.'

His aunt shrugs. 'Help yourself. I have some smashing mystery novels upstairs too. You should give those a read. Great for the soul.'

But Barnabus isn't interested in mystery novels.

CHAPTER FOURTEEN

A BIT OF LIGHT READING

ack in his bedroom Barnabus coughs and waves away a cloud of dust. He is going through the collection of old books, jars and other things stuffed into the trunk. He picks up the first book, which has a pale-green triangle on the cover, and reads the title: *Your Wrangler and You.* The next is *Dangerous Deposits,* and then *The Art of Gold-Sniffing.* There are more slim volumes underneath and a few jars with dried-up things inside, except for one which has a roll of material. Opening it, Barnabus takes out a strip of old, yellowing lace, like something you'd see on the collar of a schoolchild in Victorian times. It's so fragile it tears in his hands.

'Oops.'

Dropping the lace back into the trunk, he picks up an old, folded envelope that smells sour, like it's been soaked in milk and left to curdle in the sun. Inside is a golden coin, and Barnabus realises it is the coin that has the sour scent – hot tar smothered in curdled milk. Strange.

He wrinkles his nose, then sits on the floor, wrapped in a blanket with a glowing oil lamp nearby, and begins to read from the pile of books.

Selected excerpts from *The Art of Gold-Sniffing* by Tremenda Whifflebaum:

From Chapter 1: The Truth About Gold

Vital, exciting, and often perilous, the art of gold-sniffing is coveted by many but practised by few. The ability to smell gold is a trait passed down through bloodlines, and at the time of this book's writing there is only one family known to possess it. The ability has the potential to make its owner very rich, or (far more importantly) to keep the world turning. Gold-sniffers who devote themselves to the service of humankind and the Clock-work are admired as having made great sacrifice, but the truth is that gold-sniffers live fantastically thrilling lives. Chasing that delicate scent across continents is a never-ending adventure.

Forget the brassy stuff used to make rings and chains and watches that people on the Earth's surface wear every day. Real gold – *true* gold – is a sneaky divil of a thing that cannot be found by the average human being. It is cunning and clever, hiding in the most unlikely of places. It is devious and crafty, concealing itself in highly dangerous locations. Gold may be a metal, but you'd be best to think of it as an animal – a sly fox or a slippery eel – that does not wish to be found, and takes great joy in leading its seekers astray …

Barnabus glows with the knowledge that he is no average human being. Then he grins at the thought of gold as a sneaky animal he might one day chase across the globe. How mysterious, and how exciting! He is finally a character in one of his books, contemplating a life filled with danger and adventure.

He flips through the pages and reads some more.

From Chapter 7: Refining the Scent

Most people think that having the 'Gift of the Sniff' is enough to make a gold-sniffer. This could not be further from the truth. Any fool born into the right bloodline may be able to smell gold, but without studying, training and refining their skills, they may as well be sniffing out swagglebug poop. As has been made clear in previous chapters, not all gold is created equal. A gold-sniffer must be able to tell the wheat from the chaff, the jellybeans from the pebbles, the chocolate coins from the coin-shaped cockroaches (which don't taste anywhere near as good).

The signature scent of 'hot tar' or 'burnt rubber' is common across all forms of gold, and to the unskilled smeller it overpowers any other notes. But gold is like perfume, with hidden hints of other scents, and the presence of any of these impurities indicates a deposit that is not true gold. True gold, the only type delicate enough and powerful enough to be suitable for the Clockwork, will burn a gold-sniffer's nostril hairs with its untainted whiff of searing tar.

The following are a few of the more common defects in gold, and the associated scented notes:

Musty/cloudy – a mustiness or cloudiness on top of the hot-tar scent indicates gold that will be brittle and difficult to shape

Citrus – any pleasant hint of lemon, lime or orange in fact signals something *un*pleasant – gold that will cool unevenly after smelting, forming clumps in the metal

Clove and/or honey – undertones of either scent indicate a 'bendiness', resulting in gears or wheels that stretch and give and don't keep time

Laundry detergent – this clean scent tells a story of gold that is far too soft and will dent easily

Boiled potatoes – if accompanied by a hint of butter, this scent denotes gold that will repel heat; if unaccompanied by a buttery note, this gold will likely attract hair …

Barnabus looks towards the trunk. The scent of curdled milk and hot tar still leaks from beneath the lid – the golden coin in the envelope is not true gold. *Fascinating*.

Selected lines from *Dangerous Deposits* by Dorkly Fibbs:

The 'buried' lakes of Wickyn Wells are also suspected to have rich gold deposits remaining. Of course, any gold-sniffer wishing to reach them must brave the notorious warrens, which are filled with exploding gas pockets, stinging scorpion rats, and Wickyn earwigs (which, despite their name, prefer to nest between human toes). If that weren't enough, the tunnelling winds which ripple the water of the buried lakes are said to blow hard enough to knock you off your feet.

The shrieking mountains of Villamount Weal have no such thundering winds. The stillness there apparently causes chronic heebie-jeebies, which is compounded by eerie shrieks so loud and shrill that any visitor to the mountains is risking their eardrums …

Sandquick Swamp was once the site of an alligator-themed amusement park, but when the Alligator Leather Rollercoaster plunged down a steep track, straight into the sludgy sand, and was never seen again, the amusement park was quickly closed. Rumours persist that a vein of true gold sits at the bottom of that treacherous swamp.

The Deadly Death-filled Body Bog can be found less than thirty kilometres from Sandquick Swamp. Just ... don't go there.

Barnabus's heart hammers in his chest. When he pictured a life of danger and adventure, he didn't imagine any *particular* dangers. Reading about them is unsettling enough. Living them is surely something else entirely. Barnabus has to wonder if he is really cut out for the perilous life of a gold-sniffer.

From *Slurping Slug Slime: 101 Household Uses* by Hicklemas Duggan:

Ever have one of those days? When the front door hinge is creaking, the linoleum in the kitchen is peeling up at the corners, and your skin is drier than a riddle-hog's bottom? Well, have no fear! The versatile slime of the slurping slug has any number of useful applications in the home – from the kitchen, to the bathroom, and back again. Even garden boxes can feel the benefits of ...

Barnabus can't keep his eyes open any longer. He rests his chin on his clasped hands in an effort to keep reading, but the oil lamp is burning low. The fading light and the sway of the house lull him into a deep sleep.

CHAPTER FIFTEEN

LACE MOULD

'Blustering phlegm boils! Everybody, out of bed. *Now!* And for goodness sake, tread carefully.'

Barnabus snaps awake. He is still on the floor of his bedroom in the swaying house, surrounded by books. But he also appears to be inside a tent. A tent made of yellowed Victorian lace.

'What the …?'

Aunt Jemima continues shrieking from somewhere in the house. 'Don't touch it, don't *touch* it. Out of the house, you two, careful as you can. Honestly, a hiccupy chicken in a fox-filled wood has better luck. How on *earth* did this happen?'

Barnabus looks around his room. Sweeping shrouds of lace hang everywhere – from the ceiling, the wardrobe, the window frame. It's beautiful, but the funny, muddy smell is a little unpleasant.

The bedroom door opens slowly, groaning against the lace that stretches around the jamb. Aunt Jemima pops her head in.

'You awake? Good. We have to leave the house immediately. Get up as carefully as you can, and don't touch it. If this stuff tears once, it spreads like wildfire.'

'What is it?' Barnabus asks.

'Lace mould. The last infestation took weeks to clear. Nightmarish stuff. On your feet now – slow and steady. You can get dressed if you're careful, then out of house.'

'Can I bring these books?'

Aunt Jemima sighs. 'If you must. But gently does it.'

Barnabus begins to unbutton the pyjamas Abigail lent him, then notices the yellowed lace spreading from under the lid of the trunk.

'Uh oh.'

Minutes later Barnabus, Samson and Aunt Jemima stand on the path outside the swaying house, which looks ready to burst at the seams as the yellowed lace continues to grow inside.

'Blimey,' Samson says, 'it's already spilling out the windows. Abigail's gone off to get Brixton. Shouldn't be long.'

Aunt Jemima is shaking her head and grimacing, holding a couple of satchels she has brought out with her. 'I just don't understand how we got another infestation. We were so careful.'

Barnabus gulps and taps his aunt's arm. 'I think this is my fault, Aunt Jemima. I'm really sorry. I found this bit of lace in the trunk and I ... well, it tore in my hands. I didn't know it was mould.'

'Where did you find that trunk?' his aunt asks.

'On the floor in the hall. I think the arm in the cupboard put it there.'

'That bloody cupboard!' Aunt Jemima growls. 'Always with the mischief. I've a good mind to ...'

'Does the cupboard need to come out?' says Samson.

'No, no, leave it in. The fumigation team just worked around it last time. Seems fairly spore-proof. We, however, are undoubtedly covered in spores. Millions of the invisible little things.'

'Ooh!' Samson claps his large hands. 'Best excuse for a holiday in the sun, eh? My cousin's been at me for ages to visit her – she's got a lovely place in Belize. Oh, unless you'd prefer I stick with you guys, Jem.'

'No, no, off you go. Take the holiday. Heaven knows we all deserve one.'

'Smashing!' the man replies, clapping again. 'Couple of days on the surface, that'll do me grand. Barnabus, it's been a genuine pleasure. Don't be a stranger now, will you?'

Barnabus grins, and Aunt Jemima gives Samson a stern look as he heads down the wooden trail, waving goodbye.

'I'm really sorry about the mould, Aunt Jemima,' Barnabus says.

'It's not your fault, little plum. But it does mean that while Brixton's team fumigate the house, the rest of us have got to be de-spored.'

Barnabus frowns. That sounds painful.

'How do we get de-spored?'

His aunt hands him an empty satchel for his books. 'We do a little sunbathing. Sunlight is the best killer of lace-mould spores, so it's back to the surface we go.'

* * *

Barnabus is extremely disappointed to be leaving the Clockwork already. He wishes he had never opened that trunk. But then he thinks of the books in his satchel, and of all the pages he has yet to read, and he feels less regretful.

He and Aunt Jemima walk the trails, careful not to touch any passing cars or brush against the team of fumigators, dressed head to toe in bright-white hazmat suits, as they hurry by.

The spore-covered aunt and nephew are not permitted to use a wind-up car, so the walk beyond the golden gears of the Clockwork is terribly long. They stop to rest and occasionally eat something from Aunt Jemima's satchel, but with hours to go the woman is reluctant to pause for more than a few minutes at a time.

'I know your feet must be swollen and sore with all the walking,' she says. 'Mine feel like the sunburnt bottom of a hippopotamus. But once we're on the surface, we can sit and relax for as long as you like.'

It's not until they're outside the glorious golden globe, and the lovely ticking has become distant background noise, that Barnabus finally wonders how they are to get back up to the surface at all. Surely they can't climb up one of those curling squidgy bit tunnels. That would take a lifetime.

As the golden glow of the Clockwork fades behind them, it is replaced by a pale-blue light ahead that pulses from a number of long fluorescent bulbs hanging in the great cavernous space. The baby-blue colour is very calming, but a closer look makes Barnabus pause. The bulbs are moving; a muscular bubbling along their lengths, like worms moving along the ground. But the bulbs aren't getting anywhere. They continue to hang in place.

'So,' Aunt Jemima says, 'here's where things get a little weird.'

Barnabus is mildly alarmed. He considers everything up to this point to have been more than a little weird, so Aunt Jemima's idea of weird is bound to be downright freaky.

'Getting into the Clockwork,' the woman says, 'is relatively simple. You drop through a squidgy bit into a long tunnel, and gravity does all the work. As you might imagine, getting back up is not so simple.'

'Okay,' Barnabus says, swallowing thickly.

'To make it all the way back up to the surface as quickly as possible, we travel by dangling durlish.'

'Dangling durlish?'

Aunt Jemima points to the long, blue bulbs. 'These wonderful creatures right here.'

What Barnabus's aunt goes on to describe is not for those with a weak stomach. If you would prefer to skip the next part entirely – and nobody would blame you if you did – rest assured that you will not be missing out on any major plot points.

It's a little funny that those with a weak stomach might not want to hear about travelling by dangling durlish, because when you travel by dangling durlish, you are essentially travelling *through* a weak stomach. Let me explain.

Hanging from the ceiling like living stalactites, these extraordinarily long animals have a very simple digestive system. Food goes in one end and waste comes out the other. A human being's digestive system works in a similar way but sits neatly curled up inside their belly. If stretched out in one long line, it would measure about nine metres, and it has different sections with different jobs: the mouth, the stomach, the intestines (large and small) and a few other bits and pieces. It's really quite a complicated system that can take in stuff such as apples and cake and broccoli and candy floss, and push out … well, stuff that doesn't look anything like apples and cake and broccoli and candy floss. The human digestive system is *complex*.

The digestive system of the dangling durlish, on the other hand, is *simple*. It is already stretched out in one long line – the entire length of the animal's body – and it has no sections; it is basically a tube. It breaks down food with enzymes in the way a human intestine does, but it's not nearly as effective. So the dangling durlish eats very small, light things that can be broken down easily – dust or discarded hairs from frilly moth wings, for example. Creating a vacuum with the muscular, bubbling movement along its body, the durlish opens its wide, tendril-filled mouth and sucks up food from the air like a hoover. Anything much bigger or denser than dust and hair likely won't get digested. If a durlish mouth sucked in something that looked like an apple, for instance, then its other end would poop out something that looked pretty much like an apple. Similarly, if a durlish mouth sucked in a little boy, then its other end would poop out a little boy.

Do you see why this description came with a warning? If you managed to get through the last two paragraphs without feeling queasy, then you may be able to endure the beginning of the next chapter. However, caution is advised.

CHAPTER SIXTEEN

WIDDLEWELL

Barnabus stands on a stretched sheet of springy material underneath one of the blue fluorescent bulbs.

'Will it hurt?'

'It's like a good all-over exfoliation,' his aunt replies, standing beneath the next bulb. 'Some people like it cos it's cheaper than going to a spa. Me, I like it because it's the great equaliser.'

'What do you mean?'

'I mean that no matter who you are or how much money you have, at the centre of the Earth *everyone* is dangling durlish poop.'

Barnabus can see her point, but he'd still much rather a nice, clean elevator.

'Now,' his aunt calls out, 'it'll expel you from its other

end surprisingly quickly but it's still a long way to go, so make sure you take a deep breath before you get sucked in. There will be the odd pocket of gas where you can breathe for a split second if you need to – be warned, though, it won't smell good. And you'll want to hang on tight to that satchel if you don't want to lose it.'

Directly above Barnabus the tendrils around the animal's mouth are swaying like shoelaces in a bathtub.

'Is this really the only way to travel up?'

Aunt Jemima doesn't hear. Already bouncing on the springy sheet, she yells, 'Remember, bounce, bounce, and deep breath! One, two …'

In a panic to keep up, Barnabus makes three quick bounces, forgetting to take a deep breath before he feels the powerful suction of the durlish mouth and *WHUPP* … Everything goes blue.

It is the strangest sensation; squashy and slippy and gloopy. The strong suction continues as Barnabus goes flying up the intestine of the durlish – it seems as though each of his hairs is being pulled from his head – and after a few moments his skin starts to feel weird; prickly and numb at the same time, like how your mouth feels when you eat too much pineapple. He is forced to take a breath at the first pocket of gas he comes to, and his aunt wasn't joking – the smell is horrific. He resolves not to take another for the rest of the trip, and he barely manages. Even travelling at this ferocious speed, the journey continues for quite some time. Finally, gasping for breath, Barnabus is shot from the animal's back passage several feet into the air and splashes back down into a water-logged, muddy marsh.

Nearby his aunt is plucking mucky weeds from her soaked clothes. Her face is beaming and red.

'It does leave the skin a little raw, doesn't it?' she says, taking a bottle from her satchel. 'I have some slurping slug slime here if you're the type who likes to moisturise afterwards.'

Barnabus shakes his head as Aunt Jemima smears the greenish goo on her cheeks. His skin does feel a little tender, but the slug slime does not look appealing.

'Each to their own,' his aunt says. Her feet go *schlurrp*,

schlurrp as she makes her way out of the marsh. 'This way to the village.'

* * *

Barnabus follows his aunt down a cobbled street lined with narrow buildings painted in reds and blues and yellows. It's a joyful little village, where people call hello to one another and wave at the two soaked newcomers passing by. Barnabus spots a sign for a watchmaker's shop, one for clock repairs, and another for watchmaking *and* clock repairs.

'They fix a lot of watches and clocks here,' he says.

'And music boxes, and scientific instruments, and children's toys,' Aunt Jemima replies. 'Anything that runs on a clockwork. It's their bread and butter.'

'Do the people who repair the Clockwork – the big one, I mean – do they come from here?'

'Winders. Yes, most come from Widdlewell. As did our family, originally.'

Barnabus tries to picture his relatives on these lovely,

cobbled lanes, smiling at their neighbours, waving at passersby, and he can't help grinning at the absurdity of it. The Kwerks and Widdlewell would go together like curry sauce and ice-cream.

His aunt takes him into a cosy tavern, where the bearded barkeep immediately cries out, 'Jem! What a sight you are for sore eyes. I take it you've just popped out of a durlish's bottom?'

'I have indeed, Roly. We both have. This is my nephew, Barnabus.'

The man looks down at Barnabus with unabashed curiosity.

'Is he really? Well, I'll be. Never thought I'd see any Kwerk but you in this village, Jem.' He smiles widely. 'You're very welcome to Widdlewell, young man. Home of your ancestors, eh? Can I interest you two in a bit of breakfast?'

'If you're still serving,' Aunt Jemima says. 'And a couple of towels, please. Oh, and we'll eat out back in the sunshine, if that's alright. We're here to kill off some lace-mould spores.'

Roly inhales noisily through his teeth. 'Ooh, nasty stuff that.'

The garden out back is overgrown and lovely. Barnabus has lived his whole life with the perfectly manicured lawns and regimented flowerbeds of the Big House, which make the springing wildflowers and tall, bowing grasses of the tavern garden seem carelessly fun and inviting. He sits with Aunt Jemima at a round table and eagerly removes the books from his satchel.

'There's stuff about gold-sniffing in these.' He catches Aunt Jemima's expression and quickly adds, 'I'm only reading about it. That's all.'

She peruses the titles. 'Hmm, good for a few cold, hard facts, I suppose. Me, I prefer to learn from experience. See things in the flesh. With all the bones and gristle. I find book learning never quite matches the real thing.'

Barnabus opens *Your Wrangler and You* and finds a handwritten inscription on the first page.

For Sylvia,

Though you may not live it, you may learn it.

Your friend,

Morfidius

'I think this book was my mother's,' Barnabus says.

Aunt Jemima shrugs. 'Likely. She was bookish.'

'So am I! I've got lots of books hidden in the Big House. Someone kind sends them to me in secret cos Uncle Horace doesn't like me to read. He says it leads to thinking, which is a bad thing. He burns any books he finds that aren't about business or making money.'

Barnabus suddenly goes quiet, hoping he hasn't discouraged his aunt from saying more about his mother. Just then Roly appears with a tray of cooked breakfasts, tea and orange juice. He and Aunt Jemima chat a little, and when he leaves, she has a far-off look in her eye.

'Most of the books in the house are hers,' she says, without prompting. 'No-one reads them now.'

'You mean the ones in the swaying house?' Barnabus

asks. 'But I thought Mum never left the Big House. I thought you left her behind when *you* went away.'

Aunt Jemima's gaze snaps to him and he blushes. He doesn't reveal that he was hiding inside the walls and overheard her conversation in Uncle Horace's office.

'We both left,' Aunt Jemima says. 'Together, as soon as we were of age. We swore to each other that we would never go back to that house, but Syl did. I followed only to try and convince her to leave again. She wouldn't, and for the first time in our lives we went our separate ways. It was the beginning of the end for her. Those wretched Kwerks.'

'Did they …?' Barnabus can't finish the sentence.

'Kill her?' his aunt says. 'As good as. Their rottenness killed her spirit. She got sick. Then sicker. It was like she was shrinking. By the end she was just a shrivelled, empty shell.'

Barnabus is silent. There is a flash of anger in Aunt Jemima's hard, grey eyes.

'The Kwerks may be a wicked bunch,' she says, 'but your mother knew that as well as I did. And still she went back, believing she could convince them to be *better* people. As far as I'm concerned, her fate was of her own making.'

CHAPTER SEVENTEEN

YOUR WRANGLER AND YOU

From the Introduction to *Your Wrangler and You*:
The biggest mistake you are likely to make about wrangling is thinking that you must train your wrangler. This is nonsense. Your wrangler trains *you*. Cows don't wrangle cowboys. Cowboys wrangle cows. And your wrangler wrangles you.

It's best to think of yourself as a large, stupid animal, much like a cow. I don't mean to offend – I'm sure you're a lovely person and relatively clever in your own way – but when it comes to gold-sniffing, it is the wrangler who is the real hero, the real smarts, the real brains behind it all. Since I have devoted my life to the study of these magnificent creatures, I may be somewhat biased, but I believe human beings to be extraordinarily dim when compared to the simple yet remarkable brilliance of the average wrangler.

A wrangler employs each of its seven finely tuned senses so that you can forget four of your paltry five. You don't need to see, hear, touch or taste a single thing while your wrangler is in control (which is a good thing, too, since human senses are generally far inferior in comparison). Your wrangler allows you to forget your surroundings completely and commit all your energies to your sense of smell alone. And it is this freedom that makes it possible for a gold-sniffer to do their job. The gold-sniffer may be the light that others follow, but the wrangler is the guide that leads the light through the darkness ...

... Let's talk for a minute about Drifting Woodlands. We're all afraid of them, we all avoid them, and yet they are essential for our survival. A migrating piece of forest that roams the Earth like a lost dog is an eerie enough concept, but that these patches of woodland are forever veiled in spooky mists, and filled with forlorn sounds that cannot be explained, makes them all the less appealing. The unsettled feeling that Drifting Woodlands elicit means that no person can bear to spend a significant amount of time in them for fear of being driven out of their wits. As a result, these moving woods have not been extensively studied and remain a mystery. However, though we may not understand what they are, how they move, and why they strive to keep human beings out, we do know that they are the natural habitat of that splendid animal, the wrangler. And that in order to meet your wrangler, you must brave the mist-shrouded trees of a Drifting Woodland ...

Barnabus lets the book fall into his lap. He is puzzled. He has never heard of an animal called a wrangler, and he has read *Animals, Animals and More Animals: A Guide to the World's Animals* several times (a rather large illustrated book that remains taped to the wall of an air vent back at the Big House). Is a wrangler a made-up creature? If so, why is there an entire book about it? And why hasn't the author had some fun describing what it looks like? It seems a bizarre text altogether, with far too much detail in some ways and far too little in others.

'Fancy a wander around the village?' Aunt Jemima says, emerging from the back door of the tavern.

Barnabus sighs. He'd rather have a nap, but his aunt is smiling and he doesn't want to disappoint.

'Sure.'

'Marvellous. It's a small place, but there's plenty to see. There's a couple of tourist spots I think you'll particularly like.'

A short walk later, Barnabus and his aunt are standing outside a stone hut that's shaped like a beehive, with the word 'Klockwerker' engraved above the empty doorway.

'Our ancestral home,' Aunt Jemima says. 'Cornelius Klockwerker was the last of our line to live in this place. He must have hated it. Legend has it he tried to burn it to the ground but the fire wouldn't take, so he filled the hut up with snakes instead. Not sure what that was meant to accomplish. It was more of a gesture, I think.'

'His family name was Klockwerker?' Barnabus says.

'Yes. And our name too, I guess. He shortened it to Kwerk before stealing as much gold as he could carry from the Clockwork and running off to live a new rich-filled life in Undle.'

'He doesn't sound very nice.'

'I'd say he was an absolute gargoyle, who went on to spawn generations of more gargoyles.' She looks at Barnabus and smiles. 'Except maybe for one or two lovely misfits.'

Inside, the hut is utterly bare. It seems like a very small space to live in, but it's warm and airy at the same time, and Barnabus likes the feel of the old stone walls under his fingertips.

'Maybe we should change our name back to Klock-werker,' he says.

His aunt shrugs. 'We could. Lot of paperwork though.'

The next tourist stop is at the very centre of the village; a large working model of the Clockwork which, perhaps appropriately, isn't working.

'Hmm,' Aunt Jemima says, gazing up at the golden globe balanced on a plinth. 'It used to tick for real. The gears turned and everything. It must be broken. Oh, ha! I see. Someone's started replacing the gold pieces with iron. And they've got miniature frilly moths chewing on them too. Very clever. And a bit depressing.'

'Do the moths eat the Clockwork?' Barnabus asks.

'Not the gold pieces, no. Those, they polish to a high shine. Frilly moths are actually essential to keep the golden gears healthy, but they'll chew through any other metal. So when we have to replace damaged parts with brass or iron, the moths start chewing. We keep them off as best we can, but it's yet another job with not enough people to do it, and the new gears don't tend to last long.'

'So you really need more gold.'

'We always need more gold.' Aunt Jemima scratches one of the moth models and laughs. 'It's got fluffy wings glued on and everything! Very realistic.'

They stop for sandwiches at a charming little café and then stroll some more, calling into a couple of the clock-repair shops to warm greetings from their owners. Everyone seems to know and like Aunt Jemima, and it's a pleasant change for Barnabus to feel pride for a member of his family. As evening sets in they pick up mugs of spiced hot chocolate from a kiosk, then sit on the wall at one end of the village to sip them and watch the sun go down.

'It's always baffled me why anyone would want to leave this place forever,' Aunt Jemima says. 'This village feels like home to me.'

Barnabus agrees. The hot chocolate warms his tummy, while the gentle sounds of the village warm his heart.

He spots a darkness on the horizon and cranes his neck for a better look.

'What's that?' he asks. 'That dark bit over there.'

Aunt Jemima squints in the fading light. 'Oh, that? That's a shifting wood. A bit of forest that moves.'

'You mean a Drifting Woodland?'

'If you want to call it that. They're supposedly extremely rare, but there's always one or two hanging around Widdlewell.'

Barnabus excitedly pulls the book from his satchel. 'That's where wranglers come from,' he says. 'They must be real!'

'Where what comes from?'

'Wranglers. They're supposed to help gold-sniffers. It's in one of my books, look.'

Aunt Jemima takes the book, examines the cover, and flips quickly through the pages. 'Huh. Never heard of them.'

She hands the book back and Barnabus opens it, pointing to the paragraphs he read that afternoon.

'They help gold-sniffers,' he repeats. 'And you can

only find them in one of those Drifting Woodlands.'

'If they help gold-sniffers then you don't need one, do you?' his aunt says, raising an eyebrow. 'Because you're going to a new home. A *normal* home. Besides, no-one goes into a shifting wood on purpose, they're the creepiest things on the planet. You could lose your mind in there.'

'But if I had a wrangler, the book says I could start training as a gold-sniffer. After school, I mean,' he adds quickly. 'For when I'm older.'

'I'd rather you didn't. And for all you know that book could be full of made-up nonsense. You've no idea where it came from.'

'It came from the trunk.'

The woman rolls her eyes. 'Well, there you go. That bloody cupboard, still causing trouble from miles away.'

'Morfidius Grandthumb didn't think it was non-sense. He gave that book to my mother. And she didn't think it was nonsense, cos she kept it.'

'Of course she did. Because Syl had such good judge-ment,' Aunt Jemima sneers, throwing the remainder of her hot chocolate into the grass.

The comment stings Barnabus, bringing tears to his eyes, and his aunt's face softens.

'I'm sorry,' she says, 'I don't mean to be harsh. But it is just an old book. And even if those wrangler things did exist once, they're probably extinct now.'

Barnabus feels deflated, but he perseveres. 'Don't you think a Drifting Woodland would be worth exploring anyway? I mean, they're so strange. Don't you find them interesting?'

'I do. I also find the open mouth of a crocodile inter-esting, but you won't see me climbing into one.' She puts a hand on Barnabus's shoulder. 'I know this is all new for you, and you want to jump feet first into everything. But there's time for all that, when you're older.'

Aunt Jemima watches his face until Barnabus finally nods, though he has no intention of waiting that long.

CHAPTER EIGHTEEN

A BIG SNOT

The village is quiet. Outside Barnabus's window, an owl hoots.

He and his aunt turned in shortly after dinner in the tavern, heading to their separate rooms upstairs, still a little sullen from their argument. Barnabus has spent the hours since poring over the pages of the book with the pale-green triangle on the cover, but it's frustratingly lacking in detail. The author of *Your Wrangler and You* never describes what these animals actually look like. There are a few references to 'stringy limbs' and something called a 'rudder' that is apparently 'far more effective than the rudimentary dorsal fin of a shark', but that's about it. And there's no instruction on how to find them, either. It's clear that in order to 'meet your wrangler' you must enter a Drifting Woodland, but the book gives no direction on how to find the animal once you're in there. Nearly all the chapters focus on 'building a relationship with your wrangler', 'trusting your wrangler' and 'learning to relinquish control over your own senses'. Barnabus smacks the book onto the bed, annoyed.

'You're useless,' he says. 'I'll just have to figure it out myself.'

Aunt Jemima will be furious, Barnabus has no doubt, but he decides to brave the Drifting Woodland tonight, while the moon is full and he's still more excited than afraid.

There is snoring coming from the other rooms as Barnabus quietly steps into the hallway. He makes his way downstairs and lifts the latch on the front door, slipping outside where the night air is cold and fresh. In the dark the village is still lovely, with a peaceful sleepiness and the muffled sounds of ticking from all those clock-repair shops. The owl continues to hoot nearby, as if chastising Barnabus for his naughtiness. It follows him along the cobbled laneway, flitting from rooftop to rooftop, stopping when Barnabus reaches the edge of the village. Beyond the wall, the nighttime doesn't seem so peaceful and sleepy. The Drifting Woodland is closer than it was earlier in the evening. Perhaps it knows that Barnabus is coming and means to meet him halfway. The thought is not a comforting one.

Grass rustles beneath his feet and Barnabus wishes the owl had continued to follow him into the field, so that he wouldn't be so alone. He hears something that sounds like a bird call – not an owl, but a strange, sad kind of bird – and realises it must be the forlorn sounds that the shifting woods make. He gulps and keeps moving, and soon he is close enough for the spooky mists to curl around his ankles.

It's just trees, he says to himself. *Just trees and fog.*

But he knows it isn't. That unnerving feeling described in the book – the one that keeps people out of Drifting Woodlands – is settling in his stomach like indigestion. The tall trees with blackened bark sway in the breeze, as if to say, 'Come in, Barnabus Kwerk. Come in and meet your wrangler', though there is nothing welcoming about this welcome. Barnabus grits his teeth and squares his shoulders, because he's going in anyway.

The mist is all around him now, and as Barnabus steps inside the moving patch of forest he is reminded of Great-Aunt Claudia's tomb-like room in the northeast wing of the Big House, except that instead of floor-to-ceiling black marble, he is surrounded by black tree trunks stretching from the ground to the sky.

'*Wooo–woooooo.*'

The strange, sad bird call comes from somewhere in the branches. The sensation of indigestion that at first felt as though Barnabus had eaten one too many chocolate buns, has grown into the kind of feeling you could only get from eating five bowls of ice-cream, seven slices of jammy Swiss roll, and three large red velvet cakes slathered in sickly sweet frosting. Barnabus wants to lie down (which he doesn't dare do) or leave (which he won't allow himself to do). He trudges on as the dread spreads to his chest with fiery heartburn, bringing on a ferocious bout of hiccups.

'*Hic*. I'm not leaving,' he says, as much to himself as to the woods. 'I'm not leaving, *hic*, yet.'

'*Wooo-woooooo*,' the woodland replies.

As Barnabus moves deeper and deeper into the forest, more unpleasant and fearful sensations join the indigestion. His hairs stand on end, prickling up his arms and neck as though he is perched at the very edge of a towering cliff in thundering winds. He can't catch his breath, his teeth chatter, his knees rattle, his limbs feel weak. An awful, needling fear pierces his heart, his head and his tummy. Barnabus is overwhelmed. He has to get out of this terrible place.

He curses the book that gave him too little warning of the dread-soaked Drifting Woodland, but his anger is quenched when he remembers the inscription on the first page.

For Sylvia …

His mother had held that book in her hands, her fingers had turned the pages. Barnabus pictures a face like Aunt Jemima's but with a softness in her lovely grey eyes. In his mind his mother glances up from the book with the green triangle on the cover, and says, 'I kept this for you, Barnabus. I kept all my books for you.'

The unsettled feeling that he has all over remains, but thoughts of his mother bring warmth and comfort, and Barnabus decides he can go on.

'Wooo–wooo–wooooooooo.'

The forest tries harder. It fills the air with creepiness, with eeriness, with sounds and smells and sensations that would make most people twitch and send them running. But Barnabus holds on to the image of those soft, grey eyes, and the chilling efforts of the Drifting Woodland wash over him. Feeling almost comfortable in the dense undergrowth, he looks around for … for what? He has absolutely no idea. Is he looking for a teeny, tiny insect or a great, big, blustering beast? Should he look or listen or sniff for a wrangler? Maybe he needs to climb a tree or take a dunk in a pond. Perhaps he should have brought a lasso or a trap of some kind. At a loss, Barnabus tries a polite request instead.

'Hello?' he calls out to the darkness. 'My name is Barnabus Kwerk and I'm looking for a wrangler. *My* wrangler.' He stammers. 'Oh, I don't mean that I'd own you or anything, more that we'd be partners. I want to be a gold-sniffer, you see. Is there a wrangler here who wants to search for gold with me? Hello?'

He hears only the echoes of his own voice in response. The forest bounces his words around the trees like a hail of ping pong balls. Barnabus walks, calling out for his wrangler over and over, but hours pass and nothing comes. Weary, and knowing that he should return to the tavern before sunrise, he gives up. Perhaps there's a book somewhere called *How to Find Your Wrangler.* Or perhaps wranglers are just a thing of the past, like Aunt Jemima said. Extinct and long gone.

Moments later, he hears a strange sound that isn't the forlorn bird call of the shifting woods.

'Thluurrrpp.'

Barnabus freezes. 'Hello?'

'Thupp. Thluurrrpp.'

'Hello? Hello?'

'Thupp. Thluurrrpp, thupp.'

In the moonlight, Barnabus can see something in the

branches, and he becomes worried. It doesn't look like an animal. It looks like some sort of gluey, sticky substance caught on the branches; a greeny, gluey, sticky substance. To be perfectly frank, it looks like a very large snot. A humungous snot sneezed from the nose of a giant into the canopy of the shifting woods.

'*Thluurrrpp*,' says the snot, and Barnabus's heart beats faster.

This creature doesn't have stringy limbs or anything shaped like a shark fin that might be a 'rudder'. This creature is not what Barnabus is searching for, but it appears very interested in him. Small, marble-like eyes stare him down, and the mouth underneath them ripples with smacking, sticky lips.

'*Thluurrrpp.*'

Slowly Barnabus turns to make his way out of the woods. He hears another new sound.

Shh-glup, shh-glup, shh-glup.

The giant snot is moving down the tree trunk, slipping from branch to branch, still watching the boy below.

'Oh no,' Barnabus whimpers.

He breaks into a run, hoping the snot's sticky, gloopy body can move no faster, but the sounds tell him otherwise.

Shh-glup-shh-glup-shh-glup-shh-glup.

There is a wet *whoosh*, as if someone has thrown a soaked jumper through the air like a frisbee, then another *shh-glup-shh-glup-shh-glup*. The snot is launching itself from tree to tree, agile and nimble, catching up to Barnabus as he sprints along the ground.

Shh-glup, shh-glup, shh-glup. Shh-glup, shh-glup, shh-glup.

Barnabus nears the edge of the Drifting Woodland. He can see the moon-bathed grass up ahead. He's almost there.

SHH-GLUP.

The snot smacks onto his back, sliding gloopy mucus around his waist and down his arms and legs. Barnabus shrieks as the gloop tightens, holding him fast. The creature has him.

CHAPTER NINETEEN

WHERE THE GOLD THINGS ARE

Barnabus is face down in the brush. The snot is still on his back, its gloopy bits wrapped around his limbs like shoelaces pulled tight.

'What do you want?' Barnabus moans, but the creature doesn't answer. 'I'm sorry I came into the woods. I'm sorry I bothered you. Please let me go. I'll go back to the village and I'll never come here again, I promise.'

There is a pause, then Barnabus is wrenched backwards, the snot pulling him to his feet. He waits to be released, but the gloopy bits remain tight.

'What do you want?' Barnabus asks again.

In response the gloopy laces around his right leg

tighten even further, forcing his knee to bend and lifting his foot. Barnabus wobbles as the snot places his foot back down. Then it lifts his left leg, and his right leg again, then his left, then his right, until it has him doing an unruly march on the spot.

'Stop!' Barnabus cries, but the marching goes on and on and on.

He feels like a rag doll, his upper body swinging with his steps, until the snot's laces pull tight around his arms, forcing them to join in. Like a ridiculous soldier in exaggerated parade, Barnabus marches on the spot to invisible, soundless drums.

'I don't like this!' he yells. 'Stop!'

The snot doesn't stop. Instead it marches him forward into the trees, stamping through the undergrowth.

'Stop, stop, *stop!*'

They reach the edge of the Drifting Woodland and Barnabus feels a moment of relief. Perhaps the thing just wants him out of the woods. But they cross the misty threshold and keep going, marching over the moonlit field. Barnabus wriggles against the stringy

mucus, fighting each step, but the creature is much stronger than he is. His muscles ache as the snot takes him in a zigzag pattern through the grass, playing with him like he's a mechanical toy, forcing him to leap and jump and hop and jog. As they dance in the field, Barnabus catches a glimpse of the snot over his shoulder. The creature on his back is no longer an amorphous blob of gloop. It has smoothed into a sharp triangular shape, like that of a shark fin; a pale-green shark fin.

A rudder!

Suddenly Barnabus grins. He looks down at the stringy laces working his arms and legs, and his heart nearly bursts with excitement.

Stringy limbs and a rudder!

'Are you training me?' he asks. 'Are you my wrangler?'

'*Thluurrrpp,*' the creature says, and Barnabus leaps with joy.

At least he tries to, but his body is not currently his own. Remembering the author's words from *Your Wrangler and You*, he tries to relax under the creature's control. It is exceedingly difficult. Trusting another being to move your body for you comes naturally to no-one. The wrangler jerks Barnabus's hand out to one side and the muscles in his arm tense up to resist. His feet try to replant themselves each time they are lifted.

Relax, Barnabus tells himself. *Just relax.*

But his body won't comply. So he decides to help the wrangler with his movements instead. If the animal appears to be taking him in the direction of a clump of buttercups, he heads for the buttercups. The wrangler is not impressed. It whips him towards a clump of daisies instead. When it softens his footsteps in the grass, he tries to tread gently. It makes him stamp then, smashing the rustling blades under his shoes.

'I don't understand,' Barnabus says. 'I'm trying to do what you want me to do, go where you want me to go. Isn't that the point?'

'*Thupp, thluurrrpp, thupp,*' the wrangler snaps.

It swings him roughly around and around in circles until Barnabus is so dizzy he might be sick. He squeezes his eyes shut to block out the world spinning. There is a split second when he smells something familiar, a faint thread of burnt rubber. The gold is not close. It is many, many miles away. He doesn't understand how he knows that, or how he's able to smell it at all from such a distance. Then he opens his eyes, and the delicate scent vanishes.

Your wrangler allows you to forget your surroundings completely and commit all your energies to your sense of smell alone.

'That's it!' Barnabus says. 'I have to ignore everything else and just smell. *That's* what you're for – to take care of the everything else.'

It begins to dawn on him then how correct the author was about the importance of building trust with your wrangler. The wrangler does everything for you while your brain is (in every respect but scent) switched off. The animal looks for you, it listens for you, it feels for you, it even moves for you. So how do you switch off entirely to let the wrangler do its job?

Barnabus stills himself. He closes his eyes and tries not to hear the twittering of morning birds or feel the warmth of the first rays of sunshine spilling over the horizon. Such pleasant things are difficult to ignore, especially for a boy who has only ever seen dawn from the window of his attic bedroom.

There'll be plenty of other dawns to watch, he tells himself. *For now, concentrate.*

In the Drifting Woodland, he kept the eerie sights and sounds at bay with thoughts of his mother. He wonders if the same will work for birdsong and dawn breezes. He pictures her curled up in a garden chair, another book sitting open in her lap. She gazes up at him with soft, grey eyes and a wide smile that lifts her cheeks. Barnabus sinks into the made-up memory, and bit by bit the world around him disappears. When he catches the golden thread of scent, his mother nods, and he follows it. It is far away, beyond a freezing mountain range, deep under curled roots of oak and sycamore. Barnabus lets the scent go and follows another. This one is underwater. Again, it is not close. Countless schools of gleaming fish and hungry sharks glide over it, and booming whale calls shake the tattered sails of the shipwreck that sits on top of it. Another thread leads somewhere hot, a vein of gold buried in the desert. Yet another sits so deep underground that its hot-tar scent mingles with the ever-present hint of the Clockwork at the world's centre. There are golden threads every-where, all around him, each delicate scent promising a new adventure. And there are so many adventures to have.

Barnabus comes to as if waking from a dream. He is in the village and the sun is shining brightly. The wrangler on his back has relaxed, retracting its stringy laces from his arms and legs, to cling gently to him like a snug backpack. The smooth, triangular rudder is a soft, amorphous blob once more.

'Huh,' Barnabus says.

He is standing on a rickety stack of wooden barrels at one side of the tavern. He doesn't remember crossing the field, entering the village or climbing the stack. The wrangler did it all for him while he went scent-exploring.

From inside the tavern, he hears his aunt's voice. 'Come on, Barnabus, it's getting late. You'll miss break-fast. And it's waffles this morning.'

Still balanced on a wobbling barrel, Barnabus pushes open a small window to his right and tumbles into the tavern bathroom.

'I'm coming, Aunt Jemima!'

Splashing some cold water on his face, he then hurries to his room and throws his satchel over his shoulder.

'You'd better hide in here,' he says to the wrangler, holding the satchel open. 'I don't think I'll tell Aunt Jemima about the shifting woods just yet.'

Apparently tired after its first night of work, the animal slowly complies, slipping into the satchel and swaddling the books inside.

'Thank you, by the way,' Barnabus whispers. 'That was a wonderful adventure already.'

'*Thluurrrpp*,' the wrangler replies.

CHAPTER TWENTY

GOING CAMPING

'More whipped cream?' Aunt Jemima asks, already spooning another great dollop onto Barnabus's pile of waffles. 'You'll need the energy today. We're going on a little trip.'

'What kind of trip?'

'A camping trip.'

Barnabus grins, shoving a forkful of waffle and cream into his mouth. 'I've never been camping.'

'Marvellous. It'll be an adventure, so.' Aunt Jemima's voice is also muffled by a mouthful of breakfast. 'Abigail sent a message. She's been scouting for parts and needs help with a seller who's not the easiest. His place is in the woods, so she'll meet us outside the village and we'll head there together. It'll take a couple of days.'

Barnabus swallows thickly. 'You mean the Drifting Woodland?'

His aunt snorts. 'Lord, no! The regular woods. Past the hills on the other side.' She catches his relieved expression. 'Glad to see you've gone off the idea of exploring the shifting woods.'

Barnabus smiles awkwardly with waffle in his teeth.

While Aunt Jemima collects supplies for their trip, Barnabus has the morning to himself. He sits in the grass in the tavern garden, flipping through his collection of books, laughing at the parts of *Your Wrangler and You* that now make perfect sense to him, and reading the inscription with his mother's name over and over. His wrangler slips from the satchel, purring when Barnabus gently scratches the squishy blob between the eyes. It is so finely tuned to its surroundings that it darts back into hiding seconds before Roly appears with a jug of fresh lemonade.

Aunt Jemima returns a short while later, wearing a very large rucksack (reminiscent of the one she wore to the Big House with the dismantled hang glider inside) and carrying a slightly smaller one for Barnabus.

'You can leave the satchel,' his aunt says as he struggles to settle the rucksack on his back over the strap of the smaller bag. 'It'll be safe here.'

'No,' Barnabus replies, straightening out the satchel until it finally sits comfortably. 'I'll keep it with me.'

'Hmm. Very attached to those books, aren't you?'

He doesn't reply but joins his aunt in thanking Roly and waving goodbye for now.

The same warm greetings for Aunt Jemima follow them as they make their way down the cobbled lanes of the village. A few people call specifically to Barnabus, and he is delighted to respond. Aunt Jemima or Roly must have mentioned his name to them. He is struck again by the friendliness of Widdlewell.

About a mile outside the village, they see a figure in a blue boiler suit walking towards them. Abigail grins and waves, carrying a large rucksack on her back.

'Hello!' she calls out. 'How was Widdlewell?'

'Lovely, as always,' Aunt Jemima replies. 'How was Plumbstone?'

'Full of villains and thieves. As always.'

'Charming. Are you sure you haven't had enough of dastardly types for now? We could visit Richly Worm-worth another time.'

'No,' Abigail says, shaking her head. 'Rumour has it he's got a genuine Clockwork gear – size eight and a half with n-width cogs – still in excellent shape and everything. Best to go now before he sells it on.'

'Right so. Into the woods we go then.'

They turn off the path into thick grasses, heading for the sprawling woods to the east.

'How did someone get a piece of the Clockwork?' Barnabus asks.

'Stolen,' his aunt replies. 'Next to everyday wear and tear, theft is our biggest problem.'

'This is where crugs and whurls come in,' Abigail says.

Barnabus shivers at the mention of them. He is

tempted now to tell Aunt Jemima that Greeg knew him by name. But if he tells her the truth about the prickly creature in the Clockwork, then he should also tell her the truth about the squishy creature in his satchel. And he isn't ready to do that yet. Besides, if Greeg is up to no good, he is many, many miles away, at the centre of the Earth.

'Ooh, look!' Abigail suddenly cries out. 'One-eared squirrel with a nut. Bet he's got a good story. Hope it's not *acorn*-y one.' She pauses to glance at her companions. 'Hope the squirrel doesn't tell *acorn*-y story. A *corny* story.'

'Please keep walking,' Aunt Jemima says.

'Alright.' Abigail moves on, hissing to herself with laughter.

They stop to eat in the late afternoon, enjoying thick-cut sandwiches made by Roly that morning.

'We'll find a place to camp while it's still light,' Aunt Jemima says. 'The woods will get very dark very quickly once evening sets in, so we'll put up the tents as soon as we find a good spot.'

Barnabus and Abigail nod in agreement. Barnabus is looking forward to the camping part. He'll be like those adventurers he has read about in his hidden books.

They move on and finally stop in a clearing when the early-evening sun is still golden. Despite all the walking, Barnabus finds he isn't tired in the slightest. He helps Abigail put up their individual tents and pays attention as Aunt Jemima builds a campfire. When the woman settles back on her rolled-up sleeping bag for a cushion, with the flames crackling nearby, Barnabus nods to the book in her hands and says, 'Thought you didn't like books.'

'The kind of books that try to teach you something by *reading* about it rather than *doing* it,' Aunt Jemima replies without looking up, 'I do not care for. But trashy mystery novels? Love 'em.'

'Here,' Abigail calls from halfway up a tree. 'Wanna race climbing trees while it's still light? Or what about Hide and Seek?'

Barnabus opts for Hide and Seek. He has never played before, but when he covers his eyes and starts counting, he smiles and thinks he might be awfully good at this game. Abigail has something in her pocket that's already giving her away.

CHAPTER TWENTY-ONE

HIDE AND SEEK

'How did you find me that quick?!' Abigail is frowning so hard she could hold a pencil in her furrowed brow.

Barnabus just grins in reply. The tiny golden gear in the girl's pocket is not pure gold; there's a strong whiff of citrus intruding on the scent, which makes it very easy to sniff out amongst the trees.

They continue to play as dusk settles. Barnabus can't remember ever having this much fun in his life.

'Right,' Abigail snaps, 'your turn to count again. And this time you're *never* going to find me.'

'Don't be too sure,' Barnabus says, covering his eyes.

In the fading light, it's hard to see anything at all. Barnabus sniffs once, twice, three times. Nothing so far.

He walks further into the gloom, trying to pick up the citrusy gold. He shuts his eyes to concentrate, but still there isn't the slightest hint of the piece in Abigail's pocket. She must be hiding somewhere very clever indeed. Barnabus is about to call out that she has won this round, when he remembers his satchel is still at the campsite. He runs back, following the glow from Aunt Jemima's fire, and grabs his satchel from the ground.

'Nearly time to finish up the games, Barnabus,' his aunt says, lying cosily by the fire with her novel in one hand. 'It's getting too dark for playing.'

'Okay,' Barnabus says, hurrying away.

At a safe distance, he coaxes his wrangler from the satchel, easing the blobby creature onto his back. It immediately stretches its stringy limbs to wrap Barnabus's arms and legs, and the smooth green rudder forms, resembling a shark's dorsal fin. Barnabus stills himself and needs only the barest glimpse of his mother in his mind before he is lost in a world of scent alone. Threads of gold drift in like tangled yarn, but the citrus smell springs to the fore.

'Gotchya.' Barnabus laughs.

He follows the scent until he is nearly on top of it, then coming out of his wrangler-induced haze, he cries, 'Ha! There you … are.'

Abigail is not there. He calls her name over and over, wondering if the golden piece has fallen out of her pocket.

'Funny story,' says a muted voice from somewhere nearby. 'I climbed into this deep hole to hide, and then the ground gave way, and it turns out I'm in a much deeper hole than I intended. It was *holey* unexpected. *Wholly* unexpected. Ha!'

Barnabus inches towards the voice, careful not to go tumbling into the hole himself. He finds the gap in the forest floor and kneels down at the edge. In the starlight, he can just about make out Abigail's outline below.

'Are you alright?' he calls.

'Yep,' Abigail replies. 'But I need you to throw me a vine or something.'

'I'll go get Aunt Jemima.'

'Nope. No time. This floor's not done crumbling, I can feel it.'

The girl sounds shockingly unworried as Barnabus yells 'okay!' and begins scurrying around in the under-growth, searching for something he can use as a rope. It's not until his wrangler gently taps him on the cheek that he realises he already has something. Kneeling down again at the edge, he leans forward so that the wrangler can unwrap its stringy limbs from his arms and further extend them down the hole.

'There's a couple of … ropes coming down now!' Barnabus shouts. 'Grab hold of them.'

'Ooh!' He hears Abigail's surprise. 'What are these made of, glue?'

Barnabus doesn't answer, gripping the roots at his knees to prevent himself tipping over the edge as the wrangler retracts its limbs and pulls Abigail to the sur-face. She kicks one foot onto the ledge and climbs to safety, holding fast to the wrangler's strings.

'Ow,' Barnabus says as he is pulled to the side by her weight. 'You can let go of those now.'

Abigail is on her knees, her head bent over the wrangler limbs in her hands. 'What is this stuff?'

'It's not stuff. It's … nothing.'

Barnabus tries to pull the limbs from her. They stretch even further but the ends remain in Abigail's hands, making the wrangler '*thluurrrpp*' in complaint.

'What was *that*?' the girl says.

'I said it's nothing. Let go.'

'Hmm. Jem says that sometimes a secret is like a seed in your belly,' Abigail says. 'It will sprout shoots that poke you and vines that twist you until you open your mouth and let it out. Do you think this is a seed you should throw up before it sprouts?'

Barnabus sighs. 'Fine. It's my wrangler.'

In the deepening darkness, he can't make out Abigail's expression. She says nothing but gently turns him around. She must be tickling the creature on his back because it purrs happily.

'Where did you find it?' she asks.

'In the Drifting Woodland outside Widdlewell.'

'How did you catch it?'

'I didn't, really. It caught me.'

'Are there others?'

'I didn't see any.'

'Hmm.' Abigail sits back on her hunkers for a moment, pensive. 'Well, better pop it back wherever you've been hiding it for now. Jem won't be in the best of moods tomorrow – she hates having to talk to Richly Wormworth – and she's going to be annoyed that you're doing gold-sniffer stuff. We can show her the wrangler afterwards, when she's in better form.'

Abigail hops to her feet, heading back towards the campsite.

'Wait,' Barnabus says, jogging after her. 'You know what wranglers are?'

'They're mentioned in a few old texts I've read about the Clockwork,' the girl replies. 'Always wondered if they were real. Does it have a name, by the way?'

'Em, not that I know of.'

'Are you going to give it one?'

Barnabus shakes his head. 'I don't think so. It's not my pet, so it doesn't feel right giving it a name. If wranglers have names, I'm sure it's got one already. It just can't tell me.'

'Makes sense.' Suddenly Abigail turns to face him. 'Oh, and another thing. It probably goes without saying, but make sure the wrangler stays hidden when we get to Richly Wormworth's place. A wrangler is a kind of mythical animal from a kind of forbidden forest – a collector's dream. Richly could make a fortune from it. So if he knows you've got one, and he gets a chance to snatch it, he will.'

The wrangler slips inside the satchel and Barnabus holds it close.

CHAPTER TWENTY-TWO

RICHLY WORMWORTH

'*T*ch, tch, tch. For goodness sake … overgrown weeds … ridiculous.'

Aunt Jemima is swiping a stick at the thick undergrowth and grumbling. She has been grumbling since before breakfast.

She grumbled that her tent partially sank in a puddle during the night. She grumbled that the powdered eggs for breakfast tasted odd. She grumbled at Barnabus as he struggled to put his rucksack on over his satchel again. She grumbled that Abigail had brought them out to these bloody woods and couldn't they have gone looking for a Clockwork piece *anywhere* else? She continues to grumble as they walk, and she grumbles when they stop.

'We took a break twenty minutes ago.'

'That was two hours ago,' Abigail replies. 'We'll just stop for five minutes here. It's a nice spot with the stream and everything.'

The girl hunkers down to refill her water bottle. While Barnabus is annoyed by his aunt's mood, Abigail seems unfazed.

'Is she going to be like this all day?' he whispers, kneeling down to fill his own bottle.

'Until the visit with Richly Wormworth is over. She can't stand him. Try not to take it personally.'

Barnabus's satchel briefly dips into the water as he leans over. He snatches it to his chest to muffle the '*thluurrrpp*' from the animal inside.

'You should've left that bag in the tavern,' Aunt Jemima snaps. 'Like I told you to.'

Barnabus suppresses a retort, but it's like swallowing a stone. If his aunt snaps at him one more time, he decides, he's going to say whatever he likes.

By late afternoon, they finally reach their destination. An impossibly tall cedar tree grazes the clouds with its highest branches.

'Wormworth, Wormworth,' Aunt Jemima shrieks up at its leaves, 'let down that rusty old bucket you call an elevator!'

From midway up the massive trunk appears a face with a perfectly pomaded hairstyle and beard. The man leans out further, showing off a deep-blue housecoat glittering with embroidered silver designs.

'Jemima Kwerk,' he snorts. 'Have all my Mondays come at once?'

'Do criminals have Mondays?' she replies with scorn. 'I thought every day was Thievesday for you, Richly.'

'Ouch, Jem. Still got that spoon-sharp wit, eh?'

'A sense of humour is essential when fate continues to make jokes like you.'

'That's rich coming from a ridiculous mole rat.'

'Better than being a pompous tree lizard.'

'Spittle-filled worm raisin!'

'Gelatinous blob of squirrel droppings!'

Off to one side, Barnabus murmurs to Abigail, 'What's happening?'

'Oh, this?' she says. 'This will probably go on for a while.'

'I don't understand. Why did you ask Aunt Jemima to come if they hate each other so much? There's no way Richly will sell you the Clockwork piece now, is there?'

'A better chance than if I were on my own. I haven't anything near what a collector would pay, but he might sell it to Jem that cheap.'

'But he obviously hates her! And she hates him.'

'Seems that way, doesn't it?' Abigail says. 'You'd never guess they used to be a couple.'

'*What?*'

'Yeah, years and years ago. They were madly in love apparently.'

Barnabus watches the two adults screech at each other like seagulls fighting over a piece of toast.

'I don't believe it,' he says.

Abigail takes off her rucksack and settles herself

cross-legged on the ground. Barnabus joins her.

'Jem didn't know what Richly did for a living,' the girl says. 'You see, he calls it "dealing in antiquities". She only realised all the stuff was stolen when she recognised a gear from the Clockwork. Nearly lost her reason. That's what Samson says anyway.'

Barnabus begins to understand the foul mood that has plagued Aunt Jemima all day. 'So what happens now?' he asks.

'Well' – Abigail glances at the feuding pair – 'one of two things. Either the insults will go on until Jem storms off into the forest and we have to leave. *Or* they'll both get tired and start reminiscing about old times. And that's what we're hoping for. Cos Richly might get a bit soft then.'

Barnabus can't imagine it. His ears are ringing with the shrill cries of toast-obsessed seagulls.

'I've stuck a few horse chestnuts on strings,' Abigail says. 'Wanna play conkers?'

Barnabus nods, though he doesn't know the game. The girl pulls a number of shiny horse chestnuts from her pocket, each strung on a length of twine. She frowns for a moment, then pulls out a small golden gear and holds it up to the light. With an amused scowl on her face, she taps him hard on the nose with it.

'*That's* how you won Hide and Seek,' she says.

He blushes. 'Sorry. It was cheating, really.'

'Was it? If you'd seen me or heard me, rather than smelled me, would that have been cheating?'

Barnabus shrugs. 'Guess not.'

He doesn't fare so well with the horse chestnut game. Abigail smashes each of his with ruthless strikes from hers. So lost are they in play that it's some time before they notice the shrieking nearby has stopped. The insults continue, but in a much more civilised manner.

'... and scrambled eggs so rubbery you could've played basketball with them,' Aunt Jemima is saying, with a hint of a smile.

'At least I learned how to cook after that. Unlike you.' Richly Wormworth is leaning comfortably on the barrier that protrudes from the tree's trunk like a balcony. 'My tummy's still not right from that spiced aubergine in yellow curry.'

Tapping her foot, Aunt Jemima waves a hand. 'So are you going to lower the bucket then, or what?'

'You can enter the treehouse if you promise not to touch my stuff.'

'Your *stolen* stuff, you mean?'

'My *antiquities*,' the man says, turning a lever at his side that squeals terribly. 'You've never appreciated my line of work.'

Aunt Jemima growls as a large metal basin descends from between the cedar's branches, slowly making its way to the ground. When it finally touches down, Barnabus's aunt tips him and his rucksack inside. Abigail vaults in neatly behind him, and Aunt Jemima follows. With all three of them and the bags it's a bit of a squash, and the basin's ropes groan with effort as the group is gradually lifted into the leafy canopy.

CHAPTER TWENTY-THREE

THE TREEHOUSE

The view is spectacular. The cedar towers over most of the trees in the woods, which sit like a green carpet under the metal basin that continues to rise. From this height Barnabus can see the entire sprawling forest and beyond, to the path he and Aunt Jemima took and, very far in the distance, sunny Widdlewell. In the opposite direction is the route Abigail took to meet them, and beyond that a shadowy, purple-looking place which must be the villain-filled town of Plumbstone.

The metal basin passed the balcony on which Richly stood some time ago. He and Aunt Jemima exchanged brief insults as he continued to turn the lever and the journey went on. Now, close to the lofty top of the cedar tree, the basin is finally approaching the tree-house, though 'house' doesn't seem the right word. There appears to be an unusual growth at the top of the tree, where hundreds (perhaps even *thousands*) of branches and twigs have stretched and curled and woven together to form a giant saucer. If you've ever seen one of those circus performers who can spin a plate on the point of a stick, then you'll have a good idea of what the treehouse looks like – a massive saucer balanced on the tip of the tall trunk.

As the basin is pulled through a trapdoor in the saucer, Barnabus wonders if they're being lifted into a ginormous teacup above. He means to ask but forgets entirely as soon as they're inside the treehouse. It is magnificent. Indeed 'house' is quite the wrong word. This is a tree*mansion*.

'Woah!' he cries, as Aunt Jemima helps him clamber out of the basin. 'How did Richly build all this at the very top of a tree?'

'You'll find out soon enough,' his aunt replies. 'He'll tell you all about it. Whether you ask him to or not.'

Aunt Jemima is quite right.

'Bridget Breathlaw's Blisteringly Brilliant Branch Balm,' Richly says, grinning.

He appears several minutes after the others arrive, though Barnabus doesn't see from where. The man walks tall with his bearded chin slightly raised, cutting a very grand figure in his deep-blue velvet housecoat.

'The balm encourages wild overgrowth of tree branches,' he says, 'and when applied by a skilled and artistic hand, can be used to mould any tree into almost any shape. As you see here.'

They are in a large, circular room, lavishly furnished in deep mahogany, crimson shades and burnished gold (none of it *true* gold – Barnabus can pick up an array of intruding scents). There are archways and curved walls all around, as though the saucer is one giant maze, rather than a regular house with separate rooms. While at first astounded by the place, Barnabus's enthusiasm quickly fades. The over-the-topness of the decor is too familiar. It's much more tastefully decorated than the sitting rooms of the Big House, but any member of the

Kwerk family would gladly put their feet up on this gilded furniture.

Unrequested, Richly begins a tour of the tree-mansion, while Aunt Jemima scowls and settles herself into a comfortable armchair, whipping out her trashy mystery novel. Abigail stays with Barnabus, politely nodding and smiling at Richly's commentary, though she has obviously been here before. If the man remembers her, he pretends not to.

'Of course, I have introduced a number of tasteful pieces,' Richly is waffling on. 'The armchairs are eighteenth century Pavlovian – restored upholstery, but with original buttons. The sideboard was once owned by the Ruchwinsten family, before their kitchen-utensil empire imploded and they had to sell all their belongings. And the carved shelving is genuine Debonaire. Anything you see that is – as I like to put it – 'not nailed down', is an external piece. Everything else is built in.'

Barnabus can see the distinction. Bookshelves, countertops and a beautiful spiral staircase all emerge from the floor and walls as if they grew there – which of course they did. Much of the place is an extension of the massive saucer, twisting branches and twigs weaving upwards and outwards to make furniture and partition different areas. The spicy cedar scent wafts pleasantly throughout the tour.

'I grew this display case for the most precious of my fine china,' Richly says, pointing to a crockery-filled cabinet. 'And this console table, you'll notice, is exquisitely grown to my own design.'

'What's this?' Barnabus asks, pointing to what looks like a frozen explosion of branches in one corner.

'Oh,' Richly replies with a frown. 'That's where I spilled a bit of Branch Balm. Tripped over the Octavian rug.'

Barnabus marvels at the balm's usefulness. 'How come people don't use this Branch Balm all the time? It seems amazing.'

'It's almost impossible to get hold of,' Richly explains, 'even for someone as resourceful as myself. Some of the ingredients are, shall we say, controversial.'

'He means illegal,' Aunt Jemima's voice booms from

the centre of the maze. 'It's a crook's invention. Made *by* a criminal *for* criminals.'

'The benefits of which you very much enjoyed while you lived here, Jemima.'

'I was young then. Young and ill-informed.' There is the sound of a book snapping shut and the woman comes marching towards them. 'Enough of the pageantry, Richly. You know why we're here.'

'I can guess.'

'So where is it?'

'Is that any way to ask for a favour?' the man says, raising an eyebrow. 'I presume it is a favour you're after, and you've no intention of paying me anywhere near what the piece is worth.'

'The gear is priceless, and it belongs to the Clockwork. It belongs to *everyone*.'

'Currently,' Richly says, 'it belongs to me. But I am willing to make a deal. What meagre offerings have you brought to trade this time?'

'A selection of crawling mosses,' Abigail quickly pipes up, 'pinky nibbler bulbs, two manuscripts from

Morfidius's personal collection, the oar of a Doom Room boat that was splintered during the Great Debate of '78, and a jar of slurping slug slime.'

Richly purses his lips as though sucking on a lemon. 'A revoltingly meagre offering. Throw in a one-seventh wheel and I'll consider it.'

'We're not trading you Clockwork pieces for a Clockwork piece!' Aunt Jemima is furious.

'A *one-seventh*,' Richly says. 'A miniature wheel only. You do realise the gear you want is a size eight and a half.'

Abigail sighs. 'I have got a miniature I picked up in Plumbstone.'

'Absolutely not,' says Aunt Jemima.

'Then feel free to let yourselves down in the elevator,' says Richly, turning away. 'As always, Jem, it's been dreadful.'

He is halfway up the spiral staircase before Abigail's pleading look makes Aunt Jemima say, 'Oh for heaven's sake, alright then. You swindler.'

'I would say marvellous,' the man replies, 'but I'm the

one being swindled here.' Then he grins at Barnabus and Abigail. 'This does mean that you two get to see my finest room of all – the Treasure Nest. Brace yourselves, because it is *truly* marvellous.'

CHAPTER TWENTY-FOUR

TREASURE NEST

They follow Richly up the spiral staircase into a high-ceilinged room domed by sparkling cut glass. If the area downstairs is the teacup that rests on the tree's saucer, then Barnabus figures this room must sit like a glittery marshmallow on top. He imagines the teacup is filled with hot chocolate then, and his tummy rumbles for something sweet. It's been a while since lunchtime.

'Hmm,' Richly says, smiling at him. 'Perhaps it's time for dinner after this.'

Barnabus blushes.

The hot-tar scent of the Clockwork gear is strong, and Barnabus can tell that there are more golden things dotted about. He catches threads tainted by other smells – baby powder, seaweed, vanilla, bubblegum.

The golden gear is the biggest thing in the room, but there are other large items too. Richly points out a huge copper cauldron once owned by a trio of well-known witches, an old-fashioned penny-farthing bicycle (with its giant front wheel and an itty bitty back one) on which some princess or other cycled across the Gobi Desert for a bet, and a statue that seems to depict the fabled yeti (or abominable snowman) but is actually a likeness of famous explorer Denvi Malwen during one of his hairier phases.

While Aunt Jemima and Abigail inspect the Clockwork piece for any damage, Barnabus wanders around the other treasures. Some are banal – bits of furniture or crockery – but some are haunting and strange – pale-faced dolls, cruel-looking instruments, and a ghastly painting that seems to emit a high-pitched hum. Barnabus stops at a glass case with a very odd item inside. Stretched between two branches, the misshapen thing is papery and pale green in colour.

'You have a good eye.'

Barnabus jumps. He didn't hear Richly sneaking up behind him.

'That,' the man continues, 'is the rarest and most valuable treasure in this room. I won't be selling it any time soon. The item is unique, and therefore it is very difficult to determine its worth. I have a few of my wealthier collectors bidding already, and that will give me some idea of how much they're prepared to pay for it.'

'What is it?' Barnabus asks, not sure if he really wants to know.

Richly smiles greedily. 'That, dear child, is a mummified wrangler. It's an ancient specimen – the animals are long extinct, of course – and the only one known to exist. One of my finders spent several hours in a shifting wood to locate this beauty. Her mind suffered terribly. She was taken to hospital for extensive treatment shortly afterwards, but not before I managed to collect this exquisite thing.'

The man is still smiling, apparently untroubled by the horrors his finder went through. Horrors with which Barnabus is all too familiar.

'Will she be alright?' he asks.

'Hmm?' Richly says, finally looking away from the dried-out animal. 'Oh, who knows? But she got this out of the woods, and that's the main thing. Only thing better would have been if she'd pulled a live one out of there. Ha! Can you imagine? I could have carved it up and sold each piece for a fortune.'

An alarmed '*thluurrrpp*!' escapes Barnabus's satchel. He smacks the bag to his tummy and smiles bashfully at Richly. 'Sorry. Still hungry.'

'Of course!' the man replies. 'Where are my manners? We'll dine at once. Little girl? Jemima? Care for some dinner? I'm sure it will be a welcome break from Samson's putrid stews.' He winks at Barnabus. 'Up here among the clouds, I like to enjoy the finer things.'

Dinner is indeed fine, though Barnabus thinks it lacks the simple comfort of Samson's wholesome stew. The dining table is one of Richly's grown pieces of furniture, and it is very impressive. The chairs are high-backed and ornate, each with a plush velvet cushion. Platters of roasted meats and glazed vegetables cover the deep-green tablecloth, along with fine china and rows of silver cutlery. Though Cousin Laurel tried to teach Barnabus dinner table etiquette several times (using one of the Kwerks' electric cattle prods), Barnabus never managed to learn which fork goes with which course. He follows Aunt Jemima's example of using whichever one comes to hand.

'This is a wonderful dinner, Richly,' Abigail says. 'We're very lucky you happened to be making a feast this evening.'

'He makes a feast every evening,' says Aunt Jemima drily. 'Shocking waste of food.'

'Again,' Richly replies, 'not something you complained about when you lived here, Jem. Little girl, thank you for your compliments. I believe good food is one of the greatest joys in life, and a meal is only wasted if it is not savoured. I hope you have room for dessert. There's a twelve-layered chocolate cake in the kitchen, so decadent it'll make your head spin.'

A large cheeseboard follows dessert, which is in turn followed by coffee for the adults and a delicious hot blackcurrant drink for the children, with petit fours (those scrumptious bitesize cakes and sweets you sometimes see in fancy French pastry shops), then a glass of cognac for the adults, a glass of sparkling pear cider for the children, and a selection of wafer-thin chocolate mints.

Barnabus's tummy is like a bowling ball. A bowling ball filled with dynamite, ready to explode. He moves very carefully to the nearest armchair so as not to set it off.

'Can I interest anyone in a piece of crickle-crackle toffee?' Richly says, carrying a plate into the central room. 'It fizzles delightfully on the tongue.'

'It has always amazed me,' Aunt Jemima says, herself laid out on a deep-red fainting couch, 'how you manage to eat so much without bursting. You're like a monstrous python that can swallow a person whole.'

'The Wormworths have always been blessed with

good digestion. My grandmother consumed the entire wedding cake at my cousin's nuptials before anyone else got to it. The bride and groom were not impressed.'

Richly pops a piece of toffee into his mouth, closing his eyes as it sizzles noisily, then takes a seat with the others.

'I presume you'll want to head off shortly,' he says. 'The elevator is ready whenever you are. And I'll make the usual arrangements with my Plumbstone crew for delivery of the golden gear.' He receives only over-stuffed groans in reply. 'Unless, of course, you'd prefer to stay the night. There's plenty of room, and you're all welcome.'

Barnabus and Abigail give Aunt Jemima begging looks, and wearily she nods.

'The Maple Suite,' Richly says, directing Aunt Jemima and Abigail to one of the guest areas in the labyrinthine treemansion. 'It sleeps two and is already prepared. However, if all three of you would prefer individual rooms–'

'Don't be silly,' Aunt Jemima says. 'Abigail and I can share.'

Abigail enters the room through the home-grown archway that is without a door, and Aunt Jemima follows with both their rucksacks. Barnabus stands behind Richly, waiting to be shown to his room, when he notices the man is suddenly wearing gloves. Richly springs forward, running his hands along the branches of the open archway, which begin to move like snakes, stretching and splitting, leafy twigs sprouting, quicker and quicker, closing the door-sized gap.

'Richly?' Aunt Jemima's voice comes from within. 'What are you doing? *Richly!*'

Barnabus hears her pounding on the branches, but what was once an opening is now a wall.

'Phew!' Richly says, holding up his gloved hands to Barnabus. 'Pre-soaked in Branch Balm. That's the fastest I've ever grown anything. Pretty impressive, eh?'

'Richly!' Aunt Jemima continues to scream from behind the wall. 'You rancid pool of platypus sweat! What the hell are you doing?'

'Making money, my dear mouldy lemon peel,' Richly calls back. 'I understand that young Barnabus here was cruelly kidnapped from his family home. And there's a substantial reward for his return.'

CHAPTER TWENTY-FIVE

OUT OF THE TREE

'Richly, *please* don't do this.' Aunt Jemima's voice softens as she changes tack. 'You know how ghastly my family is. You can't send him back there. It's too cruel, even for you.'

'Cruel?' Richly says. 'Sending the boy back to a gigantic house that's drenched in precious stones and smothered in silver? Housekeepers, butlers and gardeners catering to his every need? Cruel indeed.'

'But that's just money, Richly,' Aunt Jemima pleads. 'There's no love in that house. They lock Barnabus in the attic. They treat him appallingly.'

Richly shrugs. 'If the rumours are true and the boy's got the gift, I hazard a guess they'll treat him a mite better from now on.'

There's a stunned silence from behind the branch wall. Barnabus's stomach drops into his shoes. As the youngest heir to the Kwerk fortune, Barnabus was of mild interest to his Uncle Horace. As a gold-sniffer who can make the Kwerks even richer, he is sure to become an obsession for his vile uncle and every member of that dreadful family. If they know the truth about his ability, he is doomed.

Aunt Jemima's voice is low and sorrowful. 'They'll keep him like a dog on a leash, Richly. *Please.* Don't do this.'

The man looks to Barnabus with what appears to be a sympathetic expression but shakes his head. 'What happens to my … *items* after they are sold is no concern of mine. He'll still be better off than many, Jem.'

This time Aunt Jemima switches to a more business-like tone.

'Why let them have him?' she asks. 'When you could keep him yourself. Think of it, Richly, your very own gold-sniffer. He can find you the rarest golds the world possesses. Isn't that right, Barnabus?'

Barnabus nods, but Richly is smiling and shaking his head once more. 'It's a generous offer, Jem, but we both know you'll never honour it. Besides, keeping a long-term prisoner is too far into *bad* for me. I prefer to be just a little bit *bold*.'

Aunt Jemima reverts to screaming and banging on the wall, but the noise fades for Barnabus, who has taken off at a sprint through the curling maze of the treemansion. Richly doesn't appear to be chasing him, and he feels a moment of relief when he reaches the big metal basin and jumps in. It sinks a few metres under his weight, the trapdoor underneath springing open, but then it stalls, bouncing a little with the sudden stop. Beneath him the leafy canopy is deep, dark green under the stars. Below that is the forest floor, and there is light down there, moving around. Barnabus thinks he hears shouting.

'Oh no,' he says, straining to see the sky beyond the treemansion saucer. There is light up there too, and the sound of a large bee trapped in a jar. A helicopter, getting closer. 'Oh no, oh no.'

'I'm afraid so, my dear fellow.' Richly kneels at the edge of the trapdoor, looking down at the metal basin. 'Your family have come to take you home. Now don't go shaking the elevator, that won't work. There's a trick to the mechanism that only I know. Your Aunt Gladys and I agreed to collection by helicopter, so I'm going to take you up to the walkway that circles the dome of the Treasure Nest. You'll like it up there. There's a fabulous view.'

Richly turns away to a lever that Barnabus can't see, and the basin begins to rise.

'No,' Barnabus says, his panic rising with the basin. 'No, no, no, no.'

There's a '*thluurrrpp*' at his waist and the pale-green wrangler is squeezing from his satchel. It *shh-glups* onto his back, firing its stringy limbs down his arms and legs, stretching thin as dental floss as it goes so far as to grip his fingers and feet.

'What are you doing?' Barnabus says. 'Not *now!*'

The wrangler shudders as if urging him to relinquish control.

'Not now.' Barnabus squirms against the creature's grasp. 'Let go! I can't go sniffing now.'

The basin is almost through the trapdoor, the wrangler squeezing so hard it makes Barnabus gasp for breath. The sound gets Richly's attention and he freezes, releasing the lever. The sight of the pale-green animal makes his eyes grow large as dinner plates.

'Wh-what is …?' he stammers. 'It can't be. It *can't* be.'

A terrible grin spreads across Richly's face, and Barnabus can see the man making calculations. How much money can he make from the wrangler? How much money can he make selling it off piece by piece?

Barnabus is in despair. There are wicked Kwerks on the ground below, wicked Kwerks in the sky above, and between them a wicked man ready to tear the poor animal from Barnabus's back. All is lost.

The wrangler shudders again, harder. It is so determined. The words from the book with the pale-green triangle on the cover leap to Barnabus's mind:

Your wrangler wrangles you.

The author constantly stresses the importance of

showing trust in your wrangler. So Barnabus does just that.

Richly's greedy face and clawing hands vanish into blackness, replaced by a vision of Barnabus's mother reading in the garden. Then, like a thousand thrown fishing lines, come the golden threads of scent. Barnabus picks one at random and follows it.

What happens next with Barnabus and Richly and the looming Kwerks is a fantastic feat of agility, strength and savvy, of which Barnabus is totally unaware. While he is lost in a world of scent, his wrangler demonstrates what makes wranglers so extraordinarily wonderful.

As you know by now, wranglers are more attuned to their environment than human beings can be. In addition to excellent eyesight, hearing, sense of touch, taste and smell, they can feel the tiniest flutters of electricity in the air (even the minuscule amounts produced by your heartbeat). They can also sense what is known as 'the wobble'. The wobble is a difficult thing to explain and is in no way fully understood by people. In very simple terms, it is the response of the Earth to everything that takes place in, on and around it. The ground, the air, the water, the life – every aspect of the planet, in big ways and small ways and infinitesimally teeny ways, reacts to everything else. Wranglers can feel even those infinitesimal reactions. They can tell there is someone walking on the road, around the corner a hundred metres away, because the tarmac wriggles ever, *ever* so slightly, tickled by that person's feet. They can tell that a stone in a stream has been moved, because the water is still sighing over having to change its usual route around the rocks. The wobble is an ever-printing book describing the what, the where and the how of every single thing on Earth. And it is a book that wranglers can read.

Barnabus, following the scent of a spicy gold, his body guided and moved by the wrangler, leaps from the metal basin to grab the gnarly trunk of the cedar tree. Though he has climbed out of the attic window of the Big House many times in his life, even Barnabus would struggle to crawl down such an enormously tall tree by himself, gripping only with his fingers and the toes of his shoes. But with his wrangler flexing and stretching his limbs, Barnabus moves like an acrobat, sliding and flipping and zipping towards the forest floor.

Torches flare as he nears the bottom of the trunk, and there is shouting. 'There he is! Grab him, you fools! No, not that way, *that* way. He's right above you. Look *up*, you stumbling lurch-buckets!'

Barnabus would recognise Aunt Gladys's voice if he could hear it. The wrangler hears it instead and takes evasive action.

The Barnabus–wrangler meld kicks off the tree trunk, somersaulting backwards over some very unsuspecting hired guards, and lands safely outside the circle of light around the base of the cedar tree.

'Grab him!' Aunt Gladys's voice screeches over the commotion. 'For heaven's sake, he's one little boy! If he gets away, I swear every one of you is fired!'

Barnabus never knows if Aunt Gladys's entire army of guards is fired in that forest. He continues to sniff out the spicy hot-tar scent, while his wrangler guides him through the almost total darkness of the woods.

CHAPTER TWENTY-SIX

PLUMBSTONE

We all know that there are sunny days and less sunny days, and that is true in almost every place on the planet. I say 'almost' because there is one place on Earth where the sun refuses to shine at all, no matter the day. Plumbstone is perpetually dark. The sun has turned its back on this wicked little town, and now its streets are forever murky and purple-grey.

This suits the residents of Plumbstone just fine, as wicked deeds are easier done under cover of darkness, and they have endless lists of wicked deeds to do.

There is no police force to speak of – something else that suits the Plumbstone residents well. There was briefly a Sheriff of Plumbstone, but without a deputy, or a courthouse, or a judge, or any lawyers, or anyone willing to serve on a jury or bring anyone to justice, she quickly resigned herself to a life of crime and became a pirate instead.

Piracy is a popular career path in Plumbstone – the harbour is always packed with vicious-looking ships in various states of disrepair. Thieving of all kinds is also encouraged; depending on your natural talent and how much work you're willing to put in, you can graduate from being a lowly pickpocket who steals wallets to being a cat burglar who steals diamond tiaras and has a famous nickname like 'The Ghost' or 'The Nimble Flea'.

In this gloomy town you will find con-artists, kidnappers, bootleggers, smugglers, forgers, vandals, cheats and liars, and those of an even darker disposition. Plumbstone is, as Abigail succinctly put it, a town full of villains and thieves.

And it is, unfortunately, where Barnabus finds himself when he emerges from his wrangler-induced haze. It is morning (though that's difficult to tell in a town without sunshine) and he aches all over. The wrangler must have kept him running throughout the night.

The spicy gold that Barnabus followed at random sits in the water at the bottom of the harbour, deep inside a sunken ship. Now Barnabus stands on a lonely pier, wondering which way he came into town and how he's going to get back out.

'Thank you.' He tickles the wrangler as it slinks back into his satchel. 'Poor Aunt Jemima and Abigail. How are we going to help them escape?'

He wonders if Samson has returned to the swaying house or if he's still sunning himself in Belize. Maybe Roly will know what to do, if Barnabus can find his way back to Widdlewell. He can't see any street signs though – even the roads are unfriendly in Plumbstone.

'Excuse me,' he says to a woman passing by.

But the woman just snarls and reaches for her pocket – to protect her wallet or to grab something sharp, Barnabus isn't sure. He quickly moves on.

Plumbstone is much bigger than Widdlewell, but its streets are narrower. And windier, and creepier, and darker. Barnabus is lost in a maze of alleyways. Skinny stray cats hiss at him from windowsills, and a gruff dog follows him for a while, sniffing at his satchel.

Everything is purple-grey, and shadows chase shadows over the paths and up the walls. A spidery shape makes Barnabus freeze. It's crawling up the side of a building and it's very large. *Too* large for a spider.

He's relieved when it disappears around a corner. But then he sees another, inching its way from an open window to a rooftop. And another, skittering over the ground towards a doorway. It's unsettling how quickly their long, furry legs move, whipping and gliding over the stone.

There are lots of spiders darting from dark places, avoiding the streetlamps. All with long, furry legs and (Barnabus notices with a shudder) prickly black bodies. He stays still, afraid of running into one.

'Hello, Barnabus.'

His blood runs cold, and he looks up at a huge spider clinging to the wall above him. The prickly body unfurls to reveal a sharp face with bright-blue eyes.

'Do you remember me?' the prickly spider says.

Barnabus couldn't possibly forget him.

The spiders aren't spiders after all. They're *whurls*. Each the size of a medium-sized dog, covered in hair, with a snout and a tongue hanging loosely between very sharp fangs. In shape, a whurl is like an octopus; a stout, round body with five, no, six – wait – *seven* protruding limbs. The furry limbs are extremely dexterous, moving like tentacles, sliding between the bricks of the wall, gripping tightly. And on the back of every whurl is a prickly passenger, a crug.

Greeg smiles a terrible smile.

'Blink has been *dying* to meet you,' he says.

The whurl's tongue hangs further out of her mouth, and a string of thick drool drips onto Barnabus's shoulder.

He doesn't stick around a second longer. Sprinting down an alleyway, he hears the soft *whup, whup, whup* of furry tentacles chasing after him. It's not just Blink and Greeg. Above him spidery shadows dash across building tops, catching up. There are shadows ahead too, on the ground.

Barnabus ducks into a rundown building, but the doorway on the other side is boarded up. He hides behind an old oven pulled from the wall and feels like crying. There's no way out.

Soft, furry tentacle ends pad over the floor.

'He's in here somewhere,' Greeg's voice growls. 'Spread out.'

Barnabus wonders what they'll do when they find him. What do crugs and whurls do with prisoners? Keep them? Sell them? *Eat* them?

He feels a draft on his ear. It's not a fresh draft of cool air, it's a musty draft of stale air. Most of us wouldn't notice something like that. Most of us wouldn't know what it was if we did notice it. But Barnabus isn't most of us.

Back in the Big House, with its maze of vents and hatches and forgotten, blocked-up openings, Barnabus was the clever mouse that knew every route. Spending days and weeks and months crawling through those walls, he became an expert in spotting the drafts and smells and sounds of hidden exits. Right now, he can tell there is a secret opening behind the oven. He gets his fingernails under a crack in the plaster and pulls.

The creepy whurls with their crug passengers flood the rundown building. The place is infested with furry creepy-crawlies. But they can't find the little boy they chased down the street. He has escaped.

CHAPTER TWENTY-SEVEN

BLACK CARS

Barnabus discovers that Plumbstone is much like the Big House. In a town where nobody trusts anybody, there is a ridiculous number of secret doors, false walls, hidden passages, tunnels and escape hatches. They burrow through the houses and streets as though the place is a huge, worm-eaten apple. It's a wonder the buildings are still standing.

In a dank cellar, Barnabus hears the distant sound of dripping and finds a loose stone in the wall. That stone is easily pulled out, and through the hole he reaches an old sewer. He follows the smell of stinky feet to a vent. He climbs the vent and through the grate he sees a laundry room, with baskets full of clothes so dirty they're attracting flies. Further up the vent, he feels the air getting dry. He carries on until he is in a hidden chamber above a kitchen, which leads to a secret space behind a bedroom wardrobe, which leads to a vertical hideout beside a chimney, which leads to a spiral staircase, which leads to the bottom of a well … On and on the burrows go, and Barnabus is quite enjoying being the clever mouse once more. There is the possibility that deep within the walls he will run into one or more residents of Plumbstone (these passages and doorways were made to be used, after all), but the wrangler sits happily curled over the flap of his satchel, and he knows the animal will duck back into the bag if it senses anyone coming.

Whenever he's in or under or over a road, Barnabus peers through grates and cracks in pavements, searching for spidery shadows. Since escaping through the door behind the oven, he hasn't seen even a hint of a whurl. But he has seen people on the streets. More than there were earlier. There is bustling. Excitement. Something's going on.

He spots a line of stretched black cars driving slowly

through the town, like a funeral cortège. But there is no funeral. Barnabus recognises those gleaming black cars.

The procession slows to a stop outside a rowdy pub, and Barnabus's throat tightens when a tall man in a pinstripe suit gets out.

'I'm looking for Horrida Grimm,' Uncle Horace says.

'I'm Horrida Grimm,' a woman yells from the doorway of the pub. She pulls an eye patch that rests on her forehead down over a perfectly healthy eye; the pirates of Plumbstone are nothing if not traditional. 'You the one who's promising the big money job?'

Uncle Horace frowns at the woman's eye patch and weather-beaten clothes.

'Indeed,' he says.

He snaps his fingers at his security guards, who pull two bound and gagged people from another car.

Aunt Jemima is spitting insults through the material in her mouth. Abigail is quiet, having a good look around.

A familiar bee-in-a-jar sound comes from above.

'My sisters will land in the square shortly,' Uncle Horace says to the pirate in the pub doorway. 'May we come inside? I do indeed have a business proposal to discuss. One that could be very lucrative for the villains of Plumbstone.'

* * *

The clever mouse races through hidden burrows, trying to find his way into the walls of the rowdy pub. A row of beer taps drip on Barnabus's head as he squeezes through a passage right under the bar. He makes it into the ceiling of the toilets (which is very unpleasant) and then to a small office with a large safe where the bar owner must do their accounting. Finally, he finds a back room where familiar voices make him feel queasier than the smell from the pub's toilets.

He stands in a narrow space, his back against a true wall, with a thin false wall in front. Some enterprising Plumbstoner has cut eye holes in the false wall so that Barnabus can see into the room. He doesn't know that the eyes are those of a horse in a painting. If anyone were to look closely at the watercolour horse on the wall, they would notice the animal's eyes following them about the room.

'Ms Grimm,' Uncle Horace says curtly.

'Horrida,' the woman snaps. 'Ms Grimm's my mother.'

'Very well, Horrida. I wonder if you're familiar with something called the Clockwork? It's a very large contraption positioned at the centre of the Earth.'

The woman snorts. 'You trying to be funny? We know about the Clockwork. Much better than you snooty suit types. We steal gears from it on a regular basis.'

'How would you like to steal more of those gears?' Uncle Horace smoothes his skinny moustache. 'In fact, how would you like to steal *all* of them?'

Aunt Jemima springs out of her seat, screeching through the gag in her mouth, until Aunt Gladys and Aunt Reba wrestle her back into the chair.

'Just to be clear, Ms ... Horrida,' Uncle Horace continues. 'You and your associates will be stealing the Clockwork for *me*. I will get all the gold. But you will be paid handsomely for your trouble.'

'You can't steal the whole thing,' Horrida says. 'It's

too big.'

'Piece by piece, it is possible. But it will take a large workforce, running like a factory floor. And it will require the assistance of creatures native to the Clockwork. I believe they are called crugs.'

The woman snarls. 'We don't like crugs. We won't have them in the town.'

Uncle Horace scribbles something on a piece of paper and holds it out. 'This is the amount you will be paid when the Clockwork is fully extracted.'

Horrida's one uncovered eye goes wide. 'You've got yourself a deal, pinstripe.'

'Excellent. My assistant will go through the details with you.'

The woman leaves and Aunt Reba sticks out her tongue. 'Ugh, poor people! They make my stomach turn.'

'They're a means to an end,' Uncle Horace replies.

Aunt Jemima has worked her gag loose. 'You bile-dripping wart, Horace! You dreadful crusty scab! What are you playing at?'

Uncle Horace smiles. 'I'm doing what even Great-Aunt Claudia couldn't do, Jemima. I'm doing what no Kwerk in history has *ever* done. What no Kwerk ever *dared* to do. I'm going to steal and cheat and bully and bribe until I own every single scrap of gold on this entire miserable planet.'

CHAPTER TWENTY-EIGHT

HORRIBLE HORACE

Horace Kwerk wasn't born horrible. No child is born horrible. But it's possible for a child to become horrible over time, given the right circumstances. To this end, the circumstances of the Big House in Undle could be considered perfect.

As a boy of nine or ten, Horace was quiet and eager to please. He was eager to please because whenever he *dis*pleased anyone, he was sent to the north-east wing of the house where Great-Aunt Claudia lived.

Great-Aunt Claudia was a terror. A tall woman with a towering wig of orange hair, she would lean into Horace's face spraying spittle and saying things like, 'You're useless! An insect! A dead-nosed, slimy, simpering slug!'

Then she'd turn one of her diamond nose plugs roughly in its nostril and stalk away.

It was an experience that always left young Horace feeling weak at the knees, so he tried very hard *not* to be useless. Lacking the gift of the sniff that Great-Aunt Claudia lorded over the rest of the family, he could not increase the Kwerks' already huge fortune by finding hidden deposits of gold. But he could learn everything there was to know about the family business. And he did.

Horace learned how to invest and where to invest and how to increase profits. He learned how to draw graphs and build spreadsheets and fiddle with numbers. He learned how to count money and swindle and cheat. He spent day after day alone in his room, buried in logbooks and business models and bank statements.

His younger sisters, Gladys and Reba, followed his lead, but the twins could never be taught to be serious.

'Come and play, Horace!' Jem and Syl would call to his window from the garden. 'One game of Hide and Seek. *Please!*'

Horace would shake his head and shut the window. As time went on, he'd get angry at them for being so useless, and he'd tell them so. Then the twins would taunt him instead.

'Horrible *Hor*-ace!' they'd cry from the garden. 'Horrible *Hor*-ace!'

It wasn't untrue, but it wasn't very nice either. So Horace became more angry and more serious and more horrible.

When the children grew up, Horace took over the running of the family business and the twins left the Big House and moved away.

The twins are useless, he'd say to himself. *They've never made any money for the family business. I've made lots.*

So confident was he in his success that Horace went to the north-east wing of the house with a stack of graphs and spreadsheets to prove to Great-Aunt Claudia just how much money he'd made.

The woman perused the sheets of paper while sitting on her large throne, tossing each one to the floor with a '*Pfft*'. Horace stood quietly, waiting for praise. Finally

Great-Aunt Claudia looked up.

'Useless!' she shrieked. 'Money in and money out, and not a single ounce of gold. Insects! Useless, worthless Kwerks. That's all that's left. *Useless!*'

From that day on, Horace Kwerk became about as horrible as it's possible for a person to be.

When he devised his plan to steal the Clockwork from the centre of the Earth, it was with no small amount of glee. The modern-day Kwerks have nothing to do with gold – they won't even have it in the Big House – because they can't smell it, and that makes them mad. They choose to forget the legend of Cornelius Kwerk and the great things that man did in stealing Clockwork gears and sniffing out more gold for himself. They let the Clockwork be. And truth be told, not all the Kwerks throughout history were quite as greedy or as horrible as they are now. Previous generations might have stolen a few golden gears here and there, but they weren't quite greedy enough or horrible enough to steal the entire thing and doom everybody on the planet.

Horace is that greedy. And he's certainly that horrible.

You see, he's done the maths. He's hired experts to make predictions and solve equations and add it all up.

And yes, without the Clockwork the Earth will stop turning. And yes, there'll be no night and there'll be no day and the planet will start to wither. And yes, eventually the world will end as a result.

But it won't be within Horace's lifetime. And that's the clincher.

For six or seven more glorious decades, he can live a self-satisfying life as the richest man on the planet. He will be the envy of everyone. The whole world will look to him and be jealous. He'll be able to do whatever he wants, whenever he wants, and no-one will be able to stop him. And nobody – *nobody* – will dare call him …
useless.

* * *

In the back room of the rowdy pub, Horace's mouth keeps twitching. He's itching to smile. Because he's so very clever. Half of his Grand Plan is now in motion.

Then Horace's mouth stops twitching. Because the other half of his Grand Plan is definitely *not* in motion.

When he found out that the brat, Barnabus, has the gift of the sniff, Horace was appalled. He was disgusted. He was nauseated.

Greeg, the prickly spy from the Clockwork, had relished the moment. The ghastly creature had licked his lips when he told Horace the news. And Horace couldn't hide his fury. The first Kwerk in generations to be a gold-sniffer and it's the most *useless* Kwerk of all. The injustice!

Horace had locked the door of his office and spent many hours being enraged. Incensed. *Infuriated*. Then he had emerged, calm as a cat with its claws in the mouse. Because Horace had found the silver lining on that particularly awful cloud.

Why on earth would he want the gift of the sniff? So he could travel the world sniffing out gold like a dog sniffing out a bone, or a pig sniffing out a truffle? Horace Kwerk was no dog on a leash. He was the man to *hold* the leash. He was the man to yell instructions while others did his dirty work for him. And dirty work it would most certainly be, sniffing through woods and rivers and mud.

No. Much better that the brat do it. Then all Horace would have to do is sit back and enjoy the spoils.

And that, dear reader, is where the wicked Grand Plan sprouted legs and began to run around. Because Horace realised that if he worked the brat day in and day out, he could sniff out every gold deposit left on Earth. He could sniff out every last ounce of the stuff on the surface. Then there would be mining and stealing and bribing, and eventually Horace Kwerk would own *all* the gold on the planet.

But no. There was more. Those stories Horace learned as a child and was told to forget. Stories about where the Kwerk family came from, about the massive heart of gold that ticks under everyone's feet. The *Clockwork*. Were Horace to have that too, *then* he would own all the gold on the planet. It was so simple.

And yet not so simple. Horace's mouth is now grimacing as he glares at his sisters, Gladys and Reba. Because they are utterly, gobsmackingly, hip-creakingly useless.

They let the brat escape.

CHAPTER TWENTY-NINE

SAFE INSIDE THE WALLS

In case you've forgotten, Barnabus is still hidden within the walls of the pub. He's not the eyes of the watercolour horse in the back room anymore. He followed Horrida Grimm when she left and is currently hiding in the ceiling above the bar. Had he eaten any breakfast, he would have lost it when he overheard the conversation between her and Uncle Horace. Now he is listening intently as Uncle Horace's stern-looking assistant explains the details of the Grand Plan to the woman with the eye patch. It's difficult to hear over the rowdy shouts of the pub customers, though, so Barnabus catches only bits and pieces. The crugs are involved (that explains why they and their whurls are creeping about everywhere), the whole of Plumbstone is to be hired, and there are mentions of several squidgy bits around town that are to be used.

That's good to know, Barnabus thinks. *If I can find one of those, maybe I can get down to the Clockwork and warn somebody.*

Then Barnabus hears a very interesting phrase, 'megamouth durlish'.

Since seeing the huge golden wheel in Richly Wormworth's nest of stolen treasures, Barnabus has wondered how such a large item could be brought to the surface. The narrow body of the dangling durlish through which he travelled wouldn't be nearly big enough. But a *megamouth* durlish – that sounds like a much larger animal.

The stern assistant is finished. She hands Horrida Grimm some papers and leaves. Barnabus is filled with dread.

He has to do something. But what? Aunt Jemima and Abigail would know, but they're tied up under the watchful eyes of Uncle Horace and his security guards in the back room. Samson might know, but he's sunbathing in sunny Belize. Morfidius Grandthumb might know, but he's far away in the Doom Room, and Barnabus isn't even sure if he can find a squidgy bit through which he can reach the Clockwork.

Barnabus feels hopeless. He curls up in a cubby hole above the pub's dusty chandelier and takes out his copy of *Your Wrangler and You*. From the satchel, the animal winds a comforting gluey string around Barnabus's hand as he rereads the inscription on the first page.

For Sylvia …

He wishes his mother were here. She'd know what to do.

Outside, the streets of Plumbstone are buzzing with excitement. News has spread of the filthily rich people promising a fortune to those who help steal the Clockwork. What a job! It's one that will go down in legend.

'Do the usual rules apply?' someone yells at Horrida Grimm.

'We always encourage backstabbing and cheating,' the woman replies, 'especially among friends. But I'd avoid crossing this lot in the pinstripe suits. Their reach is long, and their patience is short. Feel free to steal from each other when the job is done.'

There is one aspect of the Grand Plan about which none of the Plumbstone residents is happy: the crugs. The prickly creatures have invaded the town, and they've got their creepy, furry, tentacled pets with them. And those pets have horrible, dripping tongues that hang lazily between their terribly sharp fangs.

Usually the crugs and whurls send any stolen golden gears up through the megamouth, and the villains collect the gears at the back passage end. The crugs stay down there, and the Plumbstoners stay up here. And that's the way everyone likes it. But with so many villains to go down, and so many gears to come up, the crugs' guidance is needed underground and the whurls' strength is needed on the surface. So they've all been mashed together in one big, uncomfortable army.

Two Plumbstoners walk towards a squidgy bit in the main square. A crug and whurl pair flit about them, sometimes ahead, sometimes behind, sometimes *above*.

'Are they *trying* to give us the creeps?' one of the villains whispers to his partner.

'Definitely,' she replies, with her right hand to her face. 'We're supposed to trust them when we get down there. They say they've got a car waiting. A *car*. Whoever heard of a car at the centre of the Earth?'

'Maybe it's a trick. Maybe they're planning to eat us!'

'They probably are. Better be ready once we go through the bit.'

The woman keeps her right hand to her face. It's not voluntary. In case you're interested, hers is a tragic tale along the lines of King Midas. If you don't know the story, the greedy king wished that everything he touched would turn to gold. He got his wish. Then he couldn't eat or drink because literally *everything* he touched turned to gold.

This particular Plumbstoner was an ambitious pick-pocket. She wanted everything she touched with her right hand to stick to it. So determined was she that she slathered the hand in Bridget Breathlaw's Gloriously Gummy Glue. Then she heard an absolute shocker of a story in the local pub. Her hand flew to her face. And it never came off.

The two villains stand in the dried-up fountain in the middle of the town square. The statue of the pirate with the parrot on his shoulder is clogged up, and water no longer spews from the bird's mouth. But somehow the base of the fountain is still gloopy with mulch. It's quite springy too.

The crug perches on the edge of the fountain, her pet whurl swirling its furry tentacles.

'Right,' says the hand-faced villain, her left hand reaching for the weapon in her pocket, just in case. 'Let's get this over with.'

* * *

Barnabus is still in the ceiling of the pub, clutching the book with the inscription from Morfidius to his mother. He can't figure out what to do. He's all alone. He needs Aunt Jemima. He can't do anything by himself.

But he must. He must do *something*. So Barnabus decides to try and free Aunt Jemima and Abigail. Though he has no idea how.

He moves through the hidden passages of the pub to the back room and peers through the eye holes in the false wall. Immediately he wishes he hadn't. Aunt Jemima and Abigail are still tied up and sitting between Aunt Gladys and Aunt Reba. Uncle Horace is still there with all his formidable security guards. But two creatures have joined them.

Greeg gazes up at Uncle Horace with his bright-blue eyes.

'I appreciate your suspicion,' the crug says slyly. 'But it is true. The boy is in Plumbstone.'

Barnabus's heart hammers like a woodpecker in his chest as the prickly animal goes on.

'I'm afraid we lost him in the walls. I've come to

understand that secret passages are common in the town. He is hidden somewhere inside them.'

The terrible blue eyes are hypnotic. Barnabus holds perfectly still so as not to make a sound, but he pays no attention to the whurl beneath the crug. Blink is sniffing. Sniff, sniff, sniffing. She slinks from beneath Greeg and sniffs into the corners, under the table, under the chairs. Sniff, sniff, *SNIFF*.

Suddenly, black eyes are staring at Barnabus through the holes in the false wall. The furry creature makes a sound halfway between a squeak and a growl.

'My, my,' Greeg's voice says, 'it would appear the boy is behind that very wall. Listening in.'

'What?' cries Uncle Horace.

'Blink,' Greeg says, 'fetch.'

CHAPTER THIRTY

DOWN THE BIT

Barnabus is racing through the secret spaces of Plumbstone. But it feels as though he's moving slowly, having to squeeze through holes and climb into vents. Outside he can hear the whurl keeping up with him. Sniff, sniff, *sniff*. Sniff, sniff, *sniff*. He has to get out before those strong tentacles wriggle their way into the walls and he's trapped.

Through a storm drain he can see open ground. Barnabus doesn't waste a second. He pushes himself through the narrow space and sprints across the cobblestones. Glancing back, he sees Greeg doing an awkward hedgehog run to catch up, before somersaulting onto Blink's back. The whurl moves so fast it's frightening.

Ahead there's an old fountain with a statue of a pirate. Two people are bouncing up and down in the basin. One of them holds a hand to her face.

'Are we supposed to do it at the same time?' the man shouts.

'How should I know?' the woman calls back. 'It's not like I've been down there before.'

A crug and whurl sit on the edge of the fountain, and Greeg screeches at them, 'Grab the boy!'

Now the second whurl is running towards Barnabus. '*Thluurrrpp*,' comes a panicked sound from his satchel. The wrangler peeks out, ready to spring into action.

'No, wait!' Barnabus says. 'I know what to do.'

He grabs a book from the satchel and fires it at the charging whurl. It hits the animal on the head, knocking it and its crug to one side, and Barnabus keeps going. Straight for the fountain. Just in time to hear the familiar *schlurrp*.

Barnabus leaps into the basin and snatches the man by the ponytail.

'Ow!' the man cries. 'My hair!'

But he's already being sucked through the squidgy bit. And so is Barnabus. Everything goes black.

On his first trip through a squidgy bit, Barnabus had been terrified. He knows what to expect this time, so it's not so scary. But it is much more uncomfortable, because he and the two Plumbstoners are barrelling down the dark tunnel together. Elbows and knees are hitting faces and tummies. And as the other two are new to the experience, they are also screaming their heads off.

'Aaaagh! What is happeniiiiiing?!'

'Heeeelp meeeee!'

'If I die, don't tell my mum I stole her puuuuuurse!'

All three go hurtling from the mouth of the tunnel. Barnabus is prepared. He pushes his feet against the edges of the polished stone slide. The Plumbstoners do not. They whip around the curling antenna and fly off the end, hitting the wall and landing on the rock in a painful heap. Barnabus is already on his feet.

The crugs and whurls will be close behind, and his heart soars when he notices cars and trailers lined along the wooden path at the bottom of the steps.

'Yes!'

He races down the trail to the red car at the front of the line and begins winding its key.

'Here, you!' The woman with a hand to her face looks groggy as she stands up and yells. 'Are you our driver or something?'

Barnabus doesn't answer. Two lots of curling tentacles with prickly backs come flying from the mouth of the tunnel. They slide quickly to a stop and head for the steps.

The key is fully wound and Barnabus jumps behind the wheel. He is terrified, but there's no alternative. Releasing the brake, he catches a glimpse of furry tentacles and bright-blue eyes in the rear-view mirror before his back is slammed into the seat as the car propels forward. The blue eyes are left behind. They look furious.

* * *

A 'slip and slide' is a fun thing. You go careening down the watery inflatable slide, out of control. And if you fly off the edge it's not the end of the world because you just end up in the grass.

Being in a wind-up car going full speed on a swaying wooden path at the centre of Earth feels quite like being on a slip and slide. Except if Barnabus goes flying off the edge, it will be the end of the world. Or the end of *his* world, at least.

The car is veering all over the place. It's as if the tyres are smothered in butter. And with the car on a full wind, Barnabus can't slow it down. He can only stop or keep going. He is tempted to pull the brake suddenly and hope for the best. But he's pretty sure the best wouldn't happen, and he'd be plummeting into the cavernous dark before he had time to regret it.

On and on goes the stomach-churning ride, with Barnabus gripping the steering wheel for dear life. The warm golden globe appears in the distance and the web of crisscrossing wooden paths grows. Finally the sound of the car's engine begins to get lower in pitch. It's slowing down. When the car comes to a stop just outside the great ticking moon, Barnabus gets out and gives the key only a quarter of a full wind. This creates a much more manageable speed. As he travels through the Clockwork, he has to get out and wind the key several more times, but it's worth it to keep the car under control. Now that he's able to relax a little, he feels very grown-up and adventurous, driving a car through the heart of the Earth, escaping dangerous prickly creatures, on a mission to ... What? Save the world? But how will he do that?

When the car slows to a stop once more, Barnabus gets out and sits on the path, feeling a bit forlorn. Then he lies down on the path, with his ear muffled against the wood, feeling *very* forlorn. He needs to warn someone about Uncle Horace's awful plan. Samson, if he's back in the swaying house, and if Barnabus can find the swaying house. Or Morfidius Grandthumb, if he's still in the Doom Room, and if Barnabus can find the

Doom Room. But truth be told, the Clockwork is big and Barnabus has no idea where he is.

'I don't know how to find my way,' he whispers, and a single tear rolls down his temple onto the wood.

Being afraid is exhausting, and Barnabus has spent a whole night and day being afraid. He doesn't want to fall asleep, but he's lying down surrounded by the soothing ticking of the Clockwork, and he feels more tired than he's ever been. Without meaning to, he dozes off.

Gold, follow the, trunk, gold in the, follow the gold, trunk, in the, gold.

Barnabus snaps awake. He fell asleep. He can't believe it. The Clockwork needs saving, and he fell fast asleep.

He still has no idea where he is or what he's going to do, but he feels guilty. So he gets up to wind the car's key.

There's a shushing sound and he freezes. He hears it again, ebbing and flowing. It's what woke him, he realises. Dropping to his knees, Barnabus puts his ear to the boards. It's the whisps in the wood. What Samson calls lost whispers, according to Aunt Jemima. The shushing sound continues and Barnabus listens, and listens and listens and listens. And before long the noise begins to sound like words, repeating and gliding over each other.

Follow the gold, follow the, trunk, in the, gold in the, follow, in the trunk, follow the, in the trunk, gold.

Barnabus remembers now. There was a gold coin in the trunk where he found his mother's books, back in the swaying house. A sour-scented gold coin. Barnabus grins and opens his satchel. The animal inside looks up with marble eyes.

'Do you want to help me sniff out some gold?'

'Thluurrrpp!'

CHAPTER THIRTY-ONE

SOUNDING THE ALARM

The golden coin smells dreadful. Barnabus picks it up the moment he lets his wrangler take charge of everything except his scent.

Like really sour milk, Barnabus thinks, with a grimace.

He is following the awful stink through a lovely fog of hot tar. The pure gold of the Clockwork smells delightful to him now.

He gets closer and closer to the sour gold, and when it's still some metres away he feels the stringy limbs of the wrangler retract. The haze falls away and Barnabus is standing at the door of the swaying house. The wrangler slips back into the satchel and Barnabus pushes the door open.

The lace mould is gone, but the hall is dark. No oil lamp is lit. Barnabus's shoulders sink.

Nobody's home.

The pale, wiry arm snakes from the tall cupboard door and Barnabus gets a fright.

'Sorry,' he says, though he hadn't said his last thought out loud. 'I know you're always home. But I need help. I need Samson. My uncle's coming to steal the Clockwork, and Aunt Jemima's been kidnapped. It's a disaster.'

There are matches in a little dish by the oil lamp. Barnabus uses one to light it, nearly dropping the glass shade when the pale arm smacks on the cupboard door. It points upwards twice.

'I don't understand,' Barnabus says, glancing up at the stained wooden ceiling.

The arm walks two fingers up the edge of the cupboard, then points to the ceiling again, twice.

'Oh, upstairs,' Barnabus says. 'You mean I should go upstairs.'

The arm taps a pale finger in agreement. Barnabus wonders how mischievous the cupboard really is. Would she try to cause trouble even now, when the Clockwork is in danger? He decides not and heads up the stairs.

He sees the bedroom where he slept. The trunk is still in there and Barnabus has a look inside, suddenly remembering he lost one of his books on the surface by throwing it at a whurl. Gently fishing around the wrangler in his satchel, he smiles. It turns out he threw *Slurping Slug Slime: 101 Household Uses.* No great loss.

Barnabus picks out the golden coin from its envelope in the trunk and wrinkles his nose at the sour smell.

BANG.

He jumps to his feet. Downstairs, the cupboard impatiently smacks her hand on the door again.

'Alright, alright,' Barnabus calls. 'But I don't know what I'm looking for.'

Glancing into each of the rooms on the first floor, he is losing patience until he spots the narrow staircase at the end of the corridor that leads to an attic.

The cupboard arm had pointed twice. Up one floor, and then one more.

Barnabus climbs up to the dusty attic. In the middle of the room is a wheel with a handle, and a sign below it that reads in big red letters:

IN CASE OF <u>DIRE EMERGENCY ONLY</u>

Barnabus can't imagine a more dire emergency. He grabs the handle and begins to turn the wheel. The sound of a siren grows in the roof of the house. It's terribly loud, but Barnabus keeps turning. He keeps turning and turning until his ears are ringing and his arms are sore. Then he stands and waits as the siren dies down. When nothing happens, he goes to the circular window of the attic and looks out.

Nothing.

Barnabus is disappointed. He was hoping an army might come stomping towards the house, with weapons and tanks and fighter jets. Instead, he sees only a lonely purple car in the distance. It meanders over the wooden trails, slowing to a stop as it reaches the swaying house. Barnabus runs downstairs to see Samson climbing out of the car.

'Barnabus!' Samson throws his arms wide to give the boy a hug. 'Good to see you again so soon. Was that Jem sounding the roof alarm? Haven't heard one of those since I was a nipper. Took me a minute to figure out what the noise was.'

'I sounded the alarm,' Barnabus replies.

Samson frowns. 'Those things are for dire emergencies only, lad. Not for messing. Most people around here have never heard one before. You've probably scared the socks off anyone within earshot.'

'This *is* a dire emergency,' says Barnabus. 'Aunt Jemima's been kidnapped. So has Abigail. My family's holding them in a pub in Plumbstone. And that's not all. My uncle's coming to steal the Clockwork. *All* of it!'

The man stares at him, blanching a little.

'Are you ... Is this ... Wait, *what*?'

Some time later Barnabus waits alone outside the swaying house. He had to repeat what he knows of Uncle Horace's Grand Plan three times before Samson could believe it – the Plumbstoners coming down the squidgy bit tunnels to dismantle the Clockwork, the stolen cars that wait for them, the crugs and whurls there to assist them, and the megamouth durlish to suck each golden piece to the surface.

When it finally sunk in, Samson wound the key of the purple car as fast as he could and took off. Now Barnabus can hear an odd sound echoing through the golden gears. It's another roof siren, he realises. A second and third join it, followed by more. There must be other swaying structures with emergency alarm wheels, and the sound is spreading like fire. It's not pleasant. Deep, fret-filled notes fill the air, rattling the wooden pathways so that Barnabus can feel the worry through his feet.

When the booming sirens have died down, Barnabus spots a yellow car speeding towards the house. A blue one follows. Another blue car pulls a trailer filled with people. What looks like a gigantic centipede comes hurrying from the horizon. It gets closer and Barnabus realises it is actually a long bicycle machine with two rows of cyclists facing each other, and one person at the front to steer. There are purple cars, more yellows and blues, more megabikes and more trailers, some of which carry boats with only a handful of people inside. They're all swarming towards the swaying house like bees racing for summer's last flower. Soon the wooden trails surrounding the house are crowded with vehicles and people.

Barnabus recognises a few of those sitting in the boats that are perched on trailers. Morfidius Grandthumb and the older residents of the Doom Room look odd; pressed upon or pulled down somehow. It's as though someone painted portraits of each and then poured a glass of water over them so the paint ran.

It's the gravity, Barnabus thinks. *They're used to floating in the Doom Room. They must feel horribly heavy here.*

A purple car screeches to a halt next to Barnabus and Samson climbs out.

'Right,' the man says, out of breath. 'Everybody's in the loop now – all about your evil uncle, and the Grand Plan, and about poor Jem and Abigail. And we're all here. Everybody from the Clockwork. The whole crew. Every single one of us. So … what do we do now?'

He looks expectantly at Barnabus. Everyone does.

'Why …' Barnabus stammers. 'Why are you asking me?'

'Well,' says Samson, 'you know what's going on, don't you? You escaped and made it all the way down here to stop those wicked types from making off with the Clockwork. So you've got a plan of action, right?'

'No,' insists Barnabus. 'I came here to warn you. I thought *you'd* know what to do. Don't you have some kind of plan for emergencies?'

'Stopped doing emergency drills decades ago,' a voice shrieks from one of the boats. 'Whippersnapping eejits. I'm surprised those sirens still work.'

'You got that right, Elvira,' shouts another. 'Did away with the Protection Crews too. Served in one of them myself, once upon a day.'

'Is that true?' Barnabus asks Samson. 'You've got no plan for emergencies?'

The man shrugs uncomfortably. 'Well, yes. We barely have enough people to keep this place running as it is. The day-to-day jobs eat up all our time. We can't afford to have Protection Crews and emergency drills. We might look like a big group when we're all jam-packed here together, but the Clockwork is huge. We're a skeleton crew, really.'

'Waste of bones,' snorts Elvira.

'So what do we do now?' Barnabus asks.

He gets a terrible feeling in the pit of his stomach when nobody answers.

CHAPTER THIRTY-TWO

A BEAST OF A PLAN

The silence drags on. The people of the Clockwork are shocked, frozen like a herd of deer in headlights.

Barnabus is also in shock. Uncle Horace is coming for the Clockwork. Uncle Horace is coming for *him*. And he'll get him. Barnabus is sure of that. When there's money to be made, Horace Kwerk always gets his way.

Barnabus feels as though he is trapped once more in his attic bedroom. His family will take his wrangler and sell it to the highest bidder. They'll take his mother's books and burn them. They'll keep Aunt Jemima and Abigail prisoners forever. And when all comes to all, the Kwerks will end the world.

As he used to do in moments of distress, Barnabus retreats to the comfort of stories he has read, reliving them in his mind. He picks one of his favourites. A small village is attacked by a monster; a huge beast with horrible eyes and dripping fangs, knobbly knees and crusty toes. The villagers cannot possibly defeat a gigantic, enormous, humungous beast. Instead, they take on one bit of the beast at a time.

They set large rat-traps to snap on its crusty toes.

'Ow!' the beast howls. 'Ow!'

Then the villagers poke at its knobbly knees with pointy sticks.

'Ow, ow, ow!'

They spray shampoo in the monster's eyes.

'Ack, ack, ow!'

Then they trick the beast into gobbling up people-shaped figures made of sticky toffee.

'Nn, nn, nn!' the monster groans with its jaws stuck fast together.

It runs off into the mountains, and the villagers

cheer, 'Little by little and bit by bit, a beast is more easily beaten!'

Barnabus suddenly feels an ember burning in his belly. A fierce, defiant little ember. He climbs onto the bonnet of Samson's purple car.

'We can defeat Uncle Horace and his army of villains,' he calls out.

'But how?' says Samson.

'We take on one bit of the beast,' Barnabus replies. 'Then we take on another bit, and another bit. Until the beast is beaten.'

The crowd is still unsure, but Barnabus is not.

'You all know the Clockwork better than anyone. If you were going to steal the whole thing, where would you start?'

After a moment's pause, a voice from across the path says, 'Well, you'd have to stop the wheels from turning.'

Samson squints into the crowd and sees a woman in a grey boiler suit. 'Oh Pia, it's you,' he says. 'Stand up on a car there so we can all hear you.'

As the woman climbs onto the bonnet of a car,

Samson tells Barnabus that Pia is a winder (you might remember that a winder is someone who makes repairs to the Clockwork, and the cars, and anything else that needs repairing. Abigail is also a winder).

'I was saying,' Pia calls out, 'that if you want to remove all the gears from the Clockwork, then you have to stop them turning. That means sabotaging the Weight Stations, preventing the gleewatts from cata-pulting. Bringing everything to a halt.'

Barnabus remembers his first sight of those glorious gleewatts soaring through the air. He dreads to think what Uncle Horace's goons might do to such lovely creatures. He ponders the problem for a moment. The trail of a Weight Station curls around it like ribbon around a ball. The path is sloped, so if it were covered in oil or something slippery then maybe …

'What if we slimed the paths around each Weight Station, so the Plumbstoners would slide off?' he asks, then catches himself. 'No, no, then the gleewatts would go sliding down too.'

'Actually, that's unlikely,' says a man in a white coat.

'Gleewatt skin is smothered in minuscule suction cups. That's how they hang on to the weights. It would take more than a greasy path to send them sliding. I have a large stash of slurping slug slime that would work well.'

'A hundred and one household uses,' Barnabus says, grinning.

The man in the white coat is delighted. 'Oh, I do appreciate someone who appreciates slurping slug slime!'

Samson introduces the man as Duggan, the last biff in the Clockwork. (You might not remember that biff is short for beastie-brutey-fiendy-finder − what you might call a zoologist or a person who studies animals. If you did remember, I am impressed.)

This is great, Barnabus thinks. *One bit to take on already.*

'Next,' he says to the crowd, 'are the cars and the trailers. If the Plumbstoners do manage to stop any section of the Clockwork and get the gears off, we need to make sure that they can't get the wheels to the mega-mouth durlish and take them to the surface. So what's an easy way to break a wind-up car?'

There's a moment's pause, then Pia shouts out, 'Moth grubs!'

'Excuse me?'

'Under the paint, the outer body of our cars is made of gold, to keep the moths off. But the mechanism inside isn't. The wingless moth larvae – or grubs – are much smaller than the adults. Sometimes they'll wriggle their way in under the bonnet and start chewing. They can damage the engine pretty quick.'

'Where can we get moth grubs?' Barnabus asks.

'Ooh!' Duggan shoots his hand into the air. 'I've got plenty in the lab. And there's a number of moth nurseries around if you need more. I can show you where they are.'

'Sneak a grub into the engine over one of the front tyres,' Pia says, 'and that car won't be running for long.'

'Brilliant,' Barnabus says, thinking. 'But we will need to find the Plumbstoners and their cars before we can moth-grub them.'

'Well, that's easily done,' replies Samson. 'Winders

are always good with an ear horn. If someone's tapping on gold somewhere they shouldn't be, winders will be able to find them.'

Barnabus remembers that Abigail knew a spring in Aunt Jemima's car needed greasing, just by listening with the device that looked like the end of a small trumpet.

'Of course,' he says. 'Ear horns! Brilliant.'

Barnabus can sense a change coming over the crowd. People are excited. Saving the Clockwork doesn't sound so impossible anymore. Barnabus feels stronger than he's ever felt in his life.

CHAPTER THIRTY-THREE

How To Scare A Villain

'This is all wonderful,' Barnabus says, over-joyed that the crowd are now very enthusiastic. 'But once we've stopped the Plumbstoners from stealing the wheels, we want to make sure they leave the Clock-work. We don't want them hanging around and trying something else. How can we chase them out?'

He gazes out over the lovely people of the Clock-work and doesn't suggest they battle the Plumbstoners with wooden paddles and abseiling gear. The fiercest creatures these people face day to day are frilly moths; they wouldn't stand a chance in a fight against a horde of villains.

Just then, a little person with spirals of thick hair steps forward. 'If I may,' she says, 'scaring the pants off the villains may be the best way to get them out of the Clockwork and to keep them out.'

'Scare them how?' Barnabus asks.

'Well,' replies the woman, 'some carefully placed pinky nibblers might help to get their pulses racing.'

'Oh, that's genius, Oonagh!' cries Samson. 'Let's see how quick they run when they're in danger of losing a toe.'

Oonagh goes on. 'A few of the faster-crawling mosses can also be disconcerting for those new to the Clockwork, especially if they make it to your neck or face before you notice. They're easily flicked onto the clothes of passersby. We could use them and the nibblers to steer the Plumbstoners in the direction we want. And I might ...' She pauses here, as if for dramatic effect. 'I *might* have a few limb gulpers to place at your disposal.'

There are gasps from the crowd.

'Aren't they extinct?' Samson asks.

'Apparently not,' replies Oonagh. 'I found a patch of them thriving beyond Sector V. I'll need a few trailers and some brave hands. I can instruct a team on how to lift each plant without losing a limb.'

Bolstered by the plan taking shape, a surprising number of volunteers come forward to risk an arm or a leg in lifting the giant carnivorous limb gulpers. (And if you correctly remembered the name of Oonagh's profession as veggie-viney-weedy-zeal – veez for short, or botanist – then please reward yourself with a biscuit or other similar treat.)

'This is amazing.' The ember in Barnabus's belly has grown to a fire. 'But there's one more thing we have to do. I need a few people to come to the surface and help me rescue Aunt Jemima and Abigail from Uncle Horace. I know it's dangerous, and a bit scary, and I don't know yet how we're going to do it, but–'

'No need for trips to the surface,' Elvira pipes up from the back of her boat. 'You leave Jemima and Abigail to me.'

Barnabus doesn't want to be rude, but how can any of

the running-paint residents of the Doom Room help save his aunt and Abigail from the back room of a pub in Plumbstone?

'Don't look so worried, young whippersnapper,' says the older man sharing the woman's boat. 'Elvira's got a way with the whisps.'

The woman nods solemnly. 'They'll pass on your whispers if you time it right,' she says. 'And if you ask nicely, they'll take them all the way to the surface. If you ask *very* nicely, that is.'

Barnabus isn't convinced. Then Morfidius Grand-thumb comes forward and places a hand on his shoulder.

'Let Elvira help,' he says. 'Jem and Abigail are family to us too. We won't let them down, I promise you.'

Barnabus finally agrees but watches nervously as Morfidius gets into the car pulling Elvira's boat on a trailer.

'Somewhere quiet, Morfidius!' the woman yells as the boat manoeuvres through the crowd. 'I can't be whispering to the whisps with all this noise.'

Barnabus's chest feels tight. He hopes he isn't letting Aunt Jemima and Abigail down either.

Now that there's a plan of action, Samson begins separating the people of the Clockwork into teams – slurping slug slimers to head for the Weight Stations, winders with ear horns to track down groups of Plumbstoners, moth-grubbers to sabotage the villains' cars, and planters to set snappy traps and throw creepy mosses in suitably spooky places.

Barnabus is about to get into the purple car to help out, but he pauses and hurries back into the swaying house. He knocks on the cupboard door.

'Hello?' he says. 'I just want to thank you for telling me about the alarm wheel in the attic. Everybody's here now and we're going to try and save the Clockwork. So thanks for your help. Oh! And I never thanked you for the books in the trunk. They're brilliant. They helped me find my wrangler, and I've learned loads already about being a gold-sniffer and … and I know they were my mum's and I'm so glad to have them. You're very kind.'

He turns to head back outside.

BANG.

Barnabus doesn't jump this time. He's getting used to the cupboard's way of getting his attention.

The wiry arm is holding out what appears to be a short telescope. Barnabus takes it and closes one eye to peek inside. He sees a section of the Clockwork. Adjusting the focus wheel, he can zoom in and out; see the paths and gears up close, or see them from afar. He turns a second wheel and the image jumps to another section. He moves from glowing golden parts to sickly dark parts and gasps when he realises what the instrument is.

'It's a map! A map of the whole Clockwork. That's amazing! Thank you … um …' He doesn't feel right calling her 'cupboard' like Aunt Jemima does, so he just repeats, 'Thank you.'

The arm reaches out and gently tousles Barnabus's hair. It makes him smile, and he waits until the arm slips back inside the cupboard before he leaves.

CHAPTER THIRTY-FOUR

ON A MISSION

Pausing for a moment, Barnabus stands with one foot on the driver's seat of the car and one foot on the dashboard. He holds up his kaleidoscope map and peers through it, feeling like the captain of a ship searching for land.

The people of the Clockwork treat him like a captain. Samson gave him his own car so he can move from section to section and help out wherever he wants. (He drives at half a full wind, which is still quite fast but he's managing to keep the car on the path.) People salute him as he passes by or shout out their progress.

'Got nearly half the trail slimed here,' a woman calls as he drives past a Weight Station.

'That's brilliant!' Barnabus replies, waving.

He sneaks a look at the catapulting gleewatts. When he and the others save the Clockwork – *if* they save the Clockwork – he thinks he'll spend some time watching gleewatts. Their happiness is good for the soul.

Barnabus moves on from the Weight Station and comes across a group unloading a trailer. They wear thick gloves, and the clumps of tangled vines they are handling have mottled pink leaves and very unusual flowers – orange triangles with red tips. The triangles lunge from time to time and Barnabus can hear the *snap, snap, snap* of tiny rows of sharp teeth.

Pinky nibblers, he thinks.

He stops to ask the group if they could use his help, watching as one knotted vine is placed carefully at the edge of the wooden path, immediately curling its tendrils around the boards and nipping at its handler's glove.

'We've got the replanting here under control, thanks,' the group leader replies. 'But I think Oonagh could use a hand with the gulpers in Sector P.'

Barnabus gulps himself, but nods in agreement. He peers into his kaleidoscope map, turning the section wheel and searching for a little gold 'P' in the corner of the image. There it is. The area is dark. Not a healthy part of the Clockwork, but a clever place to put some limb gulpers. If the eerie gloom of the oily gears doesn't make the Plumbstoners uneasy, then a few terrifying arm-chomping plants should do the trick.

Barnabus meets the limb gulper team on their way to Sector P. The plants are huge, with only three fitting on each trailer. They have massive vines with mottled pink leaves, giant versions of what the pinky nibblers have, so Barnabus figures they must grip onto the wooden paths in a similar way. Instead of flowers, large bulbs hang from tall stalks, green in colour and coated in shiny pink leaves. They don't snap or move at all.

The ticking gears around the paths get darker and duller. They are entering Sector P.

'They don't seem as lively as the pinky nibblers,' Barnabus says to Oonagh as the handlers prepare to unload the plants.

'Yes,' she replies. 'They were basking in the golden hue of Sector R on the way here. It's a longer route to take, but limb gulpers get lazy and subdued in the lighter golden areas. It won't last in the dark and the grime of this sector, however. They'll get irritable. And snappy.'

The team is moving quickly. Barnabus grabs a long-handled paddle to help out, following Oonagh's instructions.

'Quickly now, very quickly,' she calls as the handlers heave one single plant off the trailer. 'Helpers, you need to be watching the bulbs, and keep those paddles at the ready. See that twitching? That's not good. If those shiny pink leaves spring wide, you're in trouble, so eyes open. Keep it moving now, nice and quick before they get grumpy.'

The plant is gently placed at the edge of the wooden path and its thick creepers grab onto the boards like a vice, some of them so long they stretch across the trail to curl around the opposite side.

'Excellent,' Oonagh says. 'Now carefully move away,

very carefully. Don't step on–'

Just then an unlucky handler trips over a stretched creeper, and the shiny leaves around one of the plant's bulbs spring apart. The green bulb splits like the mouth of a crocodile and dives towards the man now sitting on the path and …

CRUNCH.

Barnabus has shoved the end of his paddle into the bulb's mouth. The plant holds tight, shaking its bulb like a dog playing tug-of-war with its favourite toy. Barnabus can barely hold on.

'Nice catch,' Oonagh says. 'Oh, let her keep it. She'll enjoy having a little chew. And we've got paddles to spare.'

Crunch, crunch, crunch.

The limb gulper gnaws on the end of the paddle, gripping the handle with her creepers.

The other plants are carefully unloaded and placed along the path, and Oonagh shakes Barnabus's hand.

'You got us all moving when we were too frightened to think,' she says. 'I hope it's enough.'

'Me too,' Barnabus replies.

Back in his car he is a sea captain once more, peering into his kaleidoscope map to find the route back to the swaying house. Barnabus is taking the mission to save the Clockwork very seriously, but he'd be lying if he said he wasn't also having fun. Is it bad to be desperately worried and a little bit excited at the same time? He decides not. It makes him feel more empowered than afraid, which can only be a good thing.

Samson and Duggan (the biff in the white coat) are handing out moth grubs outside the swaying house. Two large containers are filled to the brim with the wriggly creatures, each the length of Barnabus's forearm. He gently places half a dozen of them into his satchel. The wrangler doesn't seem to mind the company. It tickles the grubs' tummies, and they wriggle even more.

Samson is sending those on 'moth-grubbing' detail to sectors where Plumbstoners have already been sighted. The villains were quick to invade the Clockwork. There are already dozens of them trying to dismantle parts at the edge of the golden moon. Barnabus heads for Sector U, stopping his car and continuing on foot before he even catches a glimpse of the invaders. When he is close, he can see pairs of crugs and whurls supervising the destruction. The villains have temporarily stopped the wheels by jamming things into the works, so the Weight Station for this section must still be running. The golden gears aren't happy – they creak and groan as they try to turn against the blankets and wrenches wedged between them. Cars and trailers line the nearest path, and several large wheels are already strapped in and ready for transport.

The moth grubs must sense the tension. They begin to wriggle and Barnabus taps the satchel to still them. He ducks down behind a trailer and can hear the Plumbstoners chatting as they work.

'Bloody radio,' one says, banging a walkie-talkie repeatedly against her leg. 'All I'm getting is fuzz.'

'They *told* us they wouldn't work down here,' a man snaps, glancing up at a crug before lowering his voice. 'Those prickly rats told us that. So would you stop wasting time and get that blasted harness on.'

Taking a moth grub from his bag, Barnabus tiptoes to the yellow car beyond the trailer. The villains are close, and he hunkers down. Mouthing 'good luck' to the grub, he tips it into the gap above the front tyre and the creature happily squirms inside. Within seconds there is the muted sound of teeth on metal coming from within the engine. Barnabus smiles and moves on to the next car. He grubs a blue one, then a red, another yellow and a green. This is absolutely thrilling. And very scary. He feels like the clever mouse again, scurrying behind things and under things, staying hidden as heavy boots go stomping past and golden wheels are rolled over the boards. He gets one more blue car done before he runs out of grubs. One short.

Chomp, chomp, chomp. The sound of all those moth-grub teeth is drowned out by the noise of the Plumbstoners at work. Barnabus is wondering if he can get all the way to the swaying house and back with one more grub before the villains discover the damage to their cars, when he hears a slithery voice.

'Well now.' The bright eyes of a crug stare down at Barnabus, her whurl's tentacles entwined in a gear above. 'Haven't you been naughty.'

CHAPTER THIRTY-FIVE

A WELCOME
RETURN

Had Barnabus more than a split second to think, he would naturally have jumped into the red car that does not currently have a frilly moth grub chewing on its metal insides. Unfortunately he has only a split second and instead leaps into the *nearest* car – a green one, from whose engine can be heard a muted *chomping* sound. Throwing himself over the back seat, he unhooks the trailer attached, then releases the brake. The car at least has a full wind. Which is good news and bad news.

'He was messing with the car,' the crug yells. 'Get him!'

The green car's buttery tyres slide over the boards as Barnabus swerves around trailers and cars and sprinting villains. He hears the *whizzzz whizzzz whizzzz* of other wind-up engines. With each sound behind him he wishes the green car would move a little bit faster. And with each swerve in the trail, he wishes it would move a little bit slower.

He means to head towards his own purple car, which he left behind on the path, but he is diverted down another route by the chase. Within minutes he starts to hear a *clinkety-clink-clink* in the *whizzzz* of the green car's engine.

Uh-oh.

The moth grub did fast work. Luckily, it sounds as if the Plumbstoners in pursuit are having similar problems, and their moth grubs worked even faster.

'What are you slowing down for, you fool?!'

'It's not my fault, there's something wrong with the engine.'

'Get that piece of junk off the path!'

'He's getting away!'

'Oh, popping pustules, that's mine gone too.'

'Those bloody crugs gave us broken gear. Told you they'd double-cross us.'

'Prickly snakes.'

Barnabus is hopeful as the shouting fades behind him. But there is one whizzing engine that still sounds healthy.

In his rear-view mirror, Barnabus sees the red car – the one with no moth grub eating under its bonnet – speeding towards him.

Clinkety-clink-clink-clink.

His own car is slowing.

Clinkety-clink-clink-clink-CLUNK.

It stops. Barnabus is stranded. He jumps out onto the boards, wondering what to do. The red car is still speeding towards him. It doesn't look like it's going to stop. Barnabus holds his breath and then, 'Look out beloooooooow!'

From overhead comes a large metal bird with no wings. It slams onto the wooden path, which sways with the impact, and goes squealing in the direction of the red car. Braking suddenly, the red car loses control and skids off the path. It hits one of the trails below and goes flying off that to land on another, disappearing into the spiderweb of wooden paths.

The door of the car that dropped from above opens and the driver gets out.

'I'm not too proud to admit I might have peed a little bit there. That was terrifying! Worked pretty well, though, didn't it?'

Barnabus's heart nearly bursts with joy.

'Aunt Jemima!'

'It was the oddest thing,' Aunt Jemima is saying. 'Whisps on the surface. But it's like they were in turbo mode. Abigail and I kept it together because, well, we're used to hearing them. But Horace, Gladys, Reba and all their goons started freaking out. The whisps were so loud, you see, and there were so many of them. It was like a dozen terrible choirs, all singing at once, all out of tune. It was dreadful. Truly the worst thing I've ever heard. The guards ran away screaming, leaving Abigail and me to make our escape.'

Barnabus sits happily in the passenger seat next to his aunt as they drive through the Clockwork. 'Didn't Uncle Horace try to stop you?' he asks.

'Of course, but we fought him off. I think we can safely assume his blood temperature is currently set to boil.'

Abigail isn't in the car. She and Aunt Jemima met one of the slurping slug slime teams en route and heard all about the plan to save the golden gears. They also learned that Barnabus was last seen heading for Sector U. Abigail decided to help the team slime the trails around the next Weight Station, and Aunt Jemima went in search of her nephew. Barnabus is very lucky that she found him.

'Thanks for saving me,' he says.

'If not for you,' his aunt replies, 'nobody down here would even have a clue what's going on, and the Clockwork would be toast already. So thank *you*.'

They pass several abandoned cars. Huge golden wheels are tightly strapped to the trailers attached.

'The moth-grubbing idea was genius,' Aunt Jemima says. 'I wonder where this lot went when they realised they were marooned on foot.'

It doesn't take long to find out. Aunt Jemima and Barnabus hear the commotion before they see it. Shouting and yelling, and in the midst of the noise, the snake-like voices of crugs. 'Break the catapults! Don't let them fire!'

The scene brings Barnabus to despair. The gloriously gleeful gleewatts don't look gleeful at all. They look stricken. On the trails that circle above and below him, Barnabus can see the large-bottomed creatures jostling and crowding together like the balls of a pool table tilted towards one corner, then the other. Abigail stands near the top of the trail with the rest of the sliming team. They haven't had time to complete their task, and the Plumbstoners are attacking the wooden catapults with axes and metal bars. In a panic, the gleewatts are racing from one catapult to another, desperate to find the ones that are unbroken. Very few gleewatts are soaring through the air and their lack of joy fills the space.

'We have to do something!' Barnabus cries.

Aunt Jemima grabs a long-handled paddle from a pile of moth poop nearby and says, 'I'm on it.'

She runs up the pathway, swatting at villains left, right and centre. Barnabus follows. He doesn't know what use he can be, but he won't stand there and watch while the gleewatts grow glum. He ducks under the swinging arms and growling chins of Plumbstoners, trying to knock away their axes and bars. But they are adults, too strong for him. He thinks about running to the very top of the winding trail, to help Abigail and the team spread a little more slime, but when he glances down the pathway the answer hits him. All those villains on the boards, lined up like bowling pins.

Barnabus double-checks that Aunt Jemima is on the path ahead of him, out of harm's way. Then he races to the nearest catapult that has yet to be smashed.

'Here!' he yells to all the gleewatts within earshot.

'This one is working. Look!'

He's not sure if the gleewatts can understand his words, but when he heaves up the arm of the catapult with all his might, the creatures seem to comprehend fully. They come thundering towards him from both directions, and Barnabus suddenly wonders if this was a terrible idea. He can feel the weight of the gleewatts as they bound along the trail. He'll be crushed.

A wall of heavy-bottomed bodies closes in on him, and Barnabus has no choice but to leap from the path. Almost instantly he feels the snap of gluey strings cinch around his waist and,

'Ugh!'

Barnabus dangles from the path, the wrangler's stringy limbs holding tight to the edge.

'Thank you,' Barnabus says.

'*Thupp. Thluurrrpp, thupp.*'

The entire structure trembles with the pounding of the gleewatts' feet, and Barnabus feels a little guilty as the creatures bang into each other. They are used to a bit of scuffling, however, and it is for the best. What he expects to happen does.

In the mayhem, two gleewatts are pushed from the catapult and go rolling down the path. Two giant bowling balls knocking down all those pins. Some of the Plumbstoners are smacked aside, some dive off the boards, hitting the springy sheet below or not. When the rolling gleewatts finally reach the bottom of the trail, there is a stunned silence.

There are a few villains remaining on the path above the crowded catapult, but they now look very unsure of themselves. The crugs and whurls snarl in defeat, vanishing into the golden gears and abandoning the leftover Plumbstoners.

'You're not welcome here,' Aunt Jemima declares loudly, still holding her wooden paddle. 'I suggest you leave while you still can.'

The villains escape down the trail, some of them knocked from it by the gleewatts at the working catapult, and Barnabus feels flooded with relief and delight.

CHAPTER THIRTY-SIX

SURPRISE, SURPRISE

Barnabus's delight continues. He's enjoying the speed of a car on a full wind, with Aunt Jemima at the wheel and Abigail in the back. Every sector they drive through shows more of Uncle Horace's plan falling apart. Plumbstoners race past, screaming about giant people-eating vegetables and strange cheek-grabbing mould. Some are lamenting the loss of their pinky toes.

'The nearest way out is that direction,' Aunt Jemima calls to them, pointing. 'By dangling durlish. Do us all a favour and take a big whiff on your way up.'

Other villains are drenched in slurping slug slime, having slid down the trails of Weight Stations, and more curse the back-stabbing crugs for giving them wind-up cars that wouldn't run. The crugs and whurls are nowhere to be seen. In the end, all that remains of the invasion are abandoned cars and trailers with golden wheels strapped on.

'You know, we'd better go get that car you left in Sector U,' Aunt Jemima says to Barnabus. 'There's plenty to be de-grubbed before they can be put back in rotation. In the meantime, we'll need every car that's still working.'

'And you can drop me off on the way,' Abigail says. 'Anywhere there's a team starting on repairs.'

Aunt Jemima grins. 'Isn't this marvellous?'

'Marvellous?' Barnabus says. 'It was almost a disaster!'

'But it wasn't a disaster. Good people triumphed. And that is bloody marvellous.'

They pause at a section of unmoving Clockwork, where Brixton and others are reattaching a large golden wheel and removing the junk that keeps the beautiful gears from turning. Abigail claps Barnabus on the shoulder in thanks and hops out to help with the repairs.

A little later, Barnabus is winding up the purple car in Sector U.

'I'll be giving Oonagh's group a hand,' Aunt Jemima says. 'Another good thing to come out of this mess – I'm going to see those legendary limb gulpers up close.'

'I'll come with you,' Barnabus offers.

'Take a rest, my little plum. You've earned it.' His aunt jumps behind the wheel of her car. 'If you feel like exerting yourself, you could head back to the house and stick the kettle on. We'll all be gasping for a cuppa when we get home.'

Home.

Barnabus smiles as Aunt Jemima drives off. Feeling very brave, he decides to give his own car a full wind. Well, three-quarters of a full wind. He's feeling *quite* brave.

* * *

He pulls up behind a yellow car parked outside the swaying house. Samson must be home. Barnabus wonders, with a rumbling tummy, if there's a delicious stew in the making.

'Thupp, thupp! Thluurrrpp, thupp.'

The wrangler wriggles in his satchel, and Barnabus pats the bag gently. 'Are you hungry?' he asks. 'Me too.'

But when he steps through the front door of the house, the hallway is dark.

Confused, Barnabus reaches for the matches by the oil lamp and suddenly freezes. In the gloom he can see shiny stripes across the door of the cupboard. It is duct-taped shut. A pair of bright-blue eyes at the end of the hall makes his blood run cold. Then a voice says, 'You interminable insect. Have you any idea how much money you've cost me today?'

Uncle Horace steps out from behind the front door. He is more ruffled than Barnabus has ever seen him. His pinstripe suit is wrinkled, and the jacket sits open. His greasy hair looks as though he has been roughly running his hands through it, again and again.

'It's over, Uncle Horace.' Barnabus's tummy is squirming with shock, but he stands firm. 'Your plan has failed. The Clockwork is staying where it is.'

'That much might be true,' the man says with a growl, 'but I will have my gold-sniffing dog on a leash.'

Stringy limbs erupt from Barnabus's satchel, but the whurl Blink is absurdly quick and horribly strong. She wrestles Barnabus to the ground, wrapping her muscular tentacles around the satchel and sniffing at the wrangler's limbs with interest. Greeg climbs off her back to tie Barnabus's hands and feet. The crug then duct-tapes the satchel closed as the wrangler makes worried sounds inside.

Barnabus is dragged outside and hurled onto the back seat of the yellow car, the satchel dumped next to him. He doesn't know when Aunt Jemima and the others will return to the house, and he thinks of the cupboard left behind, sealed up tightly for hours.

The yellow car whizzes along the boards with Greeg at the wheel. Blink insists on sitting next to her crug, and Uncle Horace refuses to sit in the back. As a result, the three of them are uncomfortably close in the front. With a sly grin, Blink occasionally tickles

Uncle Horace's hand or chin with a tentacle, and the thin man grimaces in disgust.

Greeg is clever and knows the Clockwork well. He takes the less populated paths, avoiding teams of winders and others when they appear in the distance. Barnabus feels the shadow of the Big House looming over him. If he doesn't escape before they reach it, he knows he never will.

'I won't do it,' he says defiantly from the back seat. 'I won't sniff out gold for you.'

'If you want to eat, you little snot,' his uncle replies, 'you'll do what you're told. Breakfast, lunch and dinner – you'll earn every meal.'

Barnabus leans his head over the side of the car to watch the wooden boards racing past. He doesn't dare jump. Even if his hands and feet weren't tied together, the car is moving far too fast. It would be a dreadful bump, and he'd very likely go rolling off the path. He slumps down in his seat and sinks into despair. He's being taken back to the way things were before. To *even worse* than the way things were before. Before, he'd been a prisoner in the Big House. Now he'd be a prisoner *and* a gold-sniffing dog on a leash. His forehead feels hot. His fingers and toes feel tingly. Barnabus's sadness is a timid green plant that suddenly blooms with fierce red flowers. The boy is furious.

'You're a rotten louse, Uncle Horace!' he bellows. 'A dreadful human being. A spittle-drenched squid.' Barnabus gasps a breath, but he's on a roll. 'You're an itchy wart on the tip of a toe. A slug in the summer salad. A great big bird plop on the windowsill. You're a gooey band-aid on the shower floor. You're a–a–a ...' He remembers a line once used by Great-Aunt Claudia. 'A *useless* waste of an ugly suit!'

Uncle Horace is stunned. He is angry and embarrassed and revolted, but there is something else creasing his thin face. Uncle Horace is a little bit afraid.

Barnabus isn't finished. The fury has reached boiling point. Tears prickle his eyeballs as he yells, 'You're the worst person who has ever lived, Uncle Horace. *And you killed my mum!*'

'What?' the man snaps. 'That's nonsense.'

Barnabus holds himself together. He doesn't want to cry. He wants to shout. 'You may not have done it with your own hands,' he yells. 'But my mother is gone because of you.'

'Don't bark at me, you little snot. It was Jemima who came and took your mother away.'

Barnabus hasn't heard that part of the story before, but it makes little difference. 'Aunt Jemima was probably trying to save her. Mum was sick. You made her sick.'

'Sick?' cries Uncle Horace. 'She was bonkers! I didn't stick her in that bloody cupboard, you wretched brat. She climbed in there herself. Climbed in one day and refused to come out.'

In a single moment, the world seems to fall away under Barnabus. It's as though he is plunging through the Clockwork gears again. A mess of feelings erupts in his chest along with that sinking, plummeting sensation. But there is no soft landing in the Doom Room this time. No landing at all. In the back of the car, Barnabus's entire body goes numb.

Mum's alive. My mum's alive.

Uncle Horace is still spitting words. 'It's an antique armoire too, worth a pretty penny. I should have made Jemima pay for it. I would have if she hadn't kicked up such a fuss. It was worth it to be rid of her. To be rid of them both. The twins have always been useless.'

Barnabus isn't listening. His mind feels ready to explode.

My mum's been here the whole time. She's been in the swaying house the WHOLE TIME.

He thinks of the wiry arm banging on the cupboard door, of the whisps sent to call him downstairs on his first night in the house, of his mother's books in the trunk and the kaleidoscope map. He thinks of the cupboard arm tousling his hair, of the made-up memory of his mother in the garden with her soft, grey eyes, and his heart breaks and mends and breaks and mends.

Why did Aunt Jemima lie?

Barnabus hooks the strap of his satchel with his fingertips and pulls it over his head. Then he leans over the side of the car once more. The Clockwork is dark all around him and the oily, blackened gears are still. It's a familiar spot. The boards are flying by so fast beneath the car. Barnabus takes a deep breath and falls out.

CHAPTER THIRTY-SEVEN

HOW THINGS END

Barnabus hits the path so hard his teeth seem to rattle in his head like dried beans in a cup. Then he is rolling, at an angle, along the trail and towards the edge. He comes to a stop, half on the boards and half off, the satchel caught underneath him. Below is a great drop through sick Clockwork gears. With tied wrists and ankles, Barnabus pushes and stretches and wobbles until he is on his feet. He remains teetering at the very edge of the path.

The yellow car screeches to a halt as soon as Barnabus topples onto the boards, but the crug and whurl stay in the front seat. It is Uncle Horace who gets out, his face screwed up in rage.

'You ungrateful worm!' he shouts, marching towards

Barnabus. 'All those years living free of charge in the Kwerk home – in *my* home – and still you'd rather jump out of a moving car than earn your keep. I should have let Jemima take you when she came for your mother.'

'I wish you had,' Barnabus replies. 'I really do.'

His uncle grabs him by the ear. 'You're coming back to the Big House, you worthless mutt.'

'No,' Barnabus says firmly. 'I'm not. You're coming with *me*.'

With his bound hands, he snatches the lapels of Uncle Horace's jacket and pushes off the path with his feet. The man's expression turns to horror as both go tumbling over the edge.

The fall is long. Uncle Horace is screaming. He grips tightly to Barnabus's ear as if it might save his life. It hurts, but Barnabus doesn't care. He closes his eyes and enjoys the ride. He has made this fall before. Last time it was filled with dread. This time it is filled with hope.

When the sensation of dropping is over, Barnabus smiles and opens his eyes. He and Uncle Horace float safely in the too-much gravity of the Doom Room. The friendly face of Morfidius Grandthumb appears nearby.

'What is this?' Uncle Horace screeches. 'What *is* this place?'

He thrashes wildly, trying to find some solid ground. But there isn't any. He screeches again, 'What is this place? Let me out. Let me out! *Immediately!*'

'Goodness me.' Morfidius's snake-like movements bring him closer to the pair. 'Those grey eyes are familiar. A little like Jem's but less pleasant. This must be the wicked uncle.'

Barnabus is enjoying his uncle's reaction to the Doom Room. 'Yes,' he replies. 'This is Uncle Horace.'

'You caused a lot of trouble, young man.' Morfidius wags a finger at Uncle Horace. 'I think it's best that you remain here, where you can do no more harm. Don't worry, the residents of the Doom Room are mostly pleasant. Their anecdotes of better days can literally go on for hours. You won't want for entertainment.'

Uncle Horace bristles. Barnabus isn't sure what offends him more – the knowledge that he may be trapped forever in this strange, floaty place, or that Morfidius dared to wag a finger and call him 'young man'.

'I see you are without a set of bellows, Barnabus,' Morfidius says, untying his hands and feet. 'I'll guide you to the ladder.'

As Barnabus drifts with the older man towards the exit, he watches Uncle Horace's pointless flailing of limbs. The occupants of several floating boats take interest.

'Who's the extra whippy whippersnapper?' Elvira's voice booms across the space.

'Whippersnapper?' Uncle Horace roars. '*Whippersnapper*? How dare you? I am Horace Kwerk. *The* Horace Kwerk. I am richer and more powerful than any of you shrivelled old raisins could possibly imagine!'

Someone lets out a long whistle. 'Ooh, he's a feisty one.'

'Kwerk?' another voice says. 'Like the old-timey

Kwerks who took off and left the Clockwork to ruin? Too lazy to do a proper day's work, that's what they were.'

'Wouldn't know what a proper day's work is, this fella,' says another.

'Let me tell you what it means to work hard, young whippersnapper. Back in *our* day ...'

Barnabus climbs the ladder, listening to Uncle Horace's fate, and smiles.

We are almost at the end of our story, dear reader, but as you know there are a few loose ends to tie up, including some very unfinished business between Barnabus and Aunt Jemima.

Barnabus is overjoyed to know that his mother is alive and (relatively) well inside the cupboard on the ground floor of the swaying house. But he is furious that his aunt kept this information from him. She let him believe that his mother was gone.

'She *is* gone,' Aunt Jemima insists, though she looks apologetic. 'I know you want to believe that Syl is still here, but there's only an empty shell in that cupboard. There's nothing of my sister left.'

They stand on a path overlooking a Weight Station, watching the gleewatts spring from catapults.

'How can you say that?' Barnabus asks. 'My mum is right here, in the swaying house. She's been here all along. She's been helping me, talking to me.'

Aunt Jemima frowns. 'She doesn't speak.'

'Maybe not with her own voice, but she sent the whisps to wake me on my first night in the Clockwork. And she gave me her books. And her map. Because she wants me to learn more about who I am and what I can do.'

Aunt Jemima lets out a deep sigh. 'It's sweet that you think so. But I spent weeks – no, *months* – trying to communicate with Syl. When I brought that awful piece of furniture to the Clockwork, I sat by it day and night, trying to coax her out. Trying to get her to say something – *anything* – to prove to me that my sister was still in there. But there was never a word, Barnabus. Not even a peep. And eventually, I gave up.'

'She's still my mum,' Barnabus presses. 'She's still here.'

'It's been years now. If Syl is really still in there, why hasn't she given me a clue? In all that time, why hasn't she let me know?'

Barnabus's voice is soft. 'Maybe when you gave up on her, she gave up on you.'

Aunt Jemima's grey eyes suddenly water and she looks away. 'Maybe.'

And that is the end of our story. Is it a sad note to finish on? Hopeful, I think.

If you're still reading, then I suspect you're one who prefers a more uplifting ending. Very well, then. Here are a few more details about what happens after Barnabus, Aunt Jemima and the others have saved the Clockwork from the wicked Kwerks.

Firstly, Aunt Jemima abandons her plans to send Barnabus to live a 'normal life' with strangers on the surface. The Clockwork becomes his home, the Doom Room his school, and Morfidius Grandthumb his teacher. (Uncle Horace has taken to playing bridge with Elvira and a few of the other Doom Room residents. He loses often and complains a lot.) Abigail is delighted to have Barnabus in the swaying house – the two have become the best of friends. Samson is also very happy about it. Barnabus's endless wonder inspires him to appreciate his work every day, even when shovelling moth poop.

Barnabus studies gold-sniffing in earnest. He and his wrangler have the most extraordinary adventures while seeking out the sneakiest, craftiest, cleverest gold on Earth. (I can't possibly relate those tales here – they would fill another book. Or maybe twenty more.) As a result, the Clockwork is becoming a much golder, much healthier place.

Barnabus's words about his mother have a strong effect on his aunt. His heart skips a beat the first time he sees Aunt Jemima park a chair next to the cupboard to sit down and read to her sister. Aunt Jemima is definitely making an effort because the chair becomes a permanent fixture in the hall, and the books change from the trashy mystery kind that Barnabus's aunt loves, to the trying-to-teach-you-something kind that his mother loves. Barnabus knows their relationship is improving when he hears them bicker.

'Honestly, Syl,' Aunt Jemima says, 'this really is the biggest load of rubbish. If they want you to learn about "fauna in the field", then the first line of the book should be, "put down this book and *go into a field*".' There's an impatient *tap-tap-tap* on the cupboard door. 'Alright, alright, I'm reading. Keep your hair on. By the way, we're doing *The Mystery of Krakenmare Manor* next week. No arguments.'

Barnabus and his mother are growing very close. Perhaps one day she'll emerge from the cupboard and speak, perhaps she won't. Barnabus doesn't mind either way. She is who she is, and he loves her.

Each night, as he lays his head down to sleep, he

hears the shushing sound of the whisps in the wall.

Goodnight, my boy, my boy, Goodnight, Goodnight, my boy, Goodnight.

And each night Barnabus rests his palm against the wall and whispers back,

"Night, Mum.'

Other Books by

Erika McGann

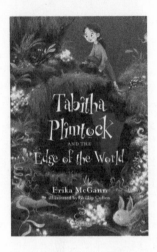

Tabitha Plimtock and the Edge of the World

Tabitha Plimtock lives in a house at the very edge of the world. Her nasty relatives send her down the cliff face to collect nuts and eggs and other stuff. But Tabitha doesn't mind, because the people who live in the wall pockets are lovely. And Mr Cratchley, who lives in the darkness down below the sunline, is the loveliest.

When rumours spread that strange creatures are climbing the wall, it's Mr Cratchley that Tabitha worries for most. Because something is stirring at the base, and it's getting very hungry ...

Find out more at obrien.ie